ANTHOLOGY

Faithless
Forgotten
Futile
Frail

The truth may set you free.

Robert Deshaies II

Copyright © 2020 Robert Deshaies II
All rights reserved
First Edition

Fulton Books, Inc.
Meadville, PA

Published by Fulton Books 2020

ISBN 978-1-64654-741-8 (paperback)
ISBN 978-1-64654-742-5 (digital)

Printed in the United States of America

Contents

Chapter 1: A Nightmare in Paris 5
Chapter 2: On the Run 21
Chapter 3: The *Trip* of a Lifetime 31
Chapter 4: Lyla Never Tells 50
Chapter 5: Is Life Worth Living Without You? 63
Chapter 6: Jungle Fever 82
Chapter 7: Funeral for a *Lover* 88
Chapter 8: Sack Lunch 104
Chapter 9: Best There Ever Was 115
Chapter 10: The Man with *the Ivory Mask* 128
Chapter 11: Blue Suite 139
Afterword: The Oddly True Story 145

Chapter 1

A Nightmare in Paris

So there I was spending my first Saturday night in Paris across the street from my creepy boss's flat. Yes, I was, in fact, smoking a cigarette.

Earlier in the week, he approached my desk and had left an overly sticky Post-it Note with an address and a poorly written description. He didn't say a word. He left a note on my desk without saying a word. The poorly written description read something like this: "Anniversaire, Cigarette, Taste." Whatever the fuck that meant? Like I said, it was a *Monday*. I had landed the night before at Charles de Gaulle, and I was exhausted. I acknowledged the note and put my head down for the rest of the week. I was kind of an introvert, but I was good at my job. I guess that was why I took the offer so quickly.

The firm had just transferred me over from New York. I was their top editor. This transfer was something of a promotion, at least that was what I thought. Yay, me. Too bad they couldn't have paid for my flight, although the flat they supplied was lovely. Anyways, the week flew by, and Saturday rolled around. It was precisely 10:04 p.m. when I entered my boss's place. The door was unlocked to his building, and thank God for the elevator. He lived on the seventh floor, and I was wearing a skintight, slim black-and-gray leather dress. Sexy, right? When choosing my outfit earlier, I hadn't set my mind to whether I was aiming to be sexy or sophisticated. So take me as you like.

The elevator opened, and my inner monologue stopped. I heard one ring, and I reached the seventh floor. I stepped out onto the level, and the porcelain floor reflected nicely against his polished piano-black doors. On his door, there was a note. This one was written quite beautifully, and it wasn't overly sticky. This note read, "Entre La Deviance." Honestly, it had just occurred to me. I have been living in Paris for a week, and I don't understand any French. Had I even ventured anywhere other than the office and my place? I grabbed the door handle, and I entered. The piano doors swung open to an entryway of mythological magnitude. Wow.

This flat was a masterpiece—porcelain floors, twilight drapes, pairing excellently with the midnight bar and bar top. Everyone attending was dressed for pleasure. It was a masquerade for some; others, well…I saw thongs and bow ties. As my eyes made their way through the densely packed room, I saw pretty much every piece of skin you could imagine. I would go no further. I wondered then if I had just stepped into some orgy, but that observation proved all too real as the night went on.

Everyone's gaze quickly darted away from me as I took my second step. I guess I wasn't worth that much attention. I kept my head down and dashed to the bar. I looked at the strapping young man serving my food and beverage and said, "Vodka Red Bull."

And he said, "Non."

"What the fuck do you mean *non*?"

With his sexy, annoyed tone, he spoke, "Mademoiselle, we have beer and wine. No alcohol."

I responded apologetically and took a glass of red. I sipped the surprisingly delicious wine and took my glass and winked at Mr. Non. Before I moved to the perfect viewing point, I wrote down my number on the cheap napkin; I don't think he would text me.

So I darted off to the window in the corner, and I decided to, quote, unquote, "people watch." It was the only activity I could think of without entering this…I still wasn't quite sure what this was. The view from up here was beautiful, at least from what I could see down the street. The higher you were in Paris seemed to be the exact place anyone would want to be. This corner, besides the splendid view, was perfect for my situation. I could have a presence without being present. The girl in the corner—absent, but present. As I cowered in my corner and sipped moderately, *albeit quite excessively*, a coworker noticed me awkwardly squeezing myself into the edges. We exchanged the firm head nod. You know, the "Hey, I work with you, but don't know your name" one. I raised my hand awkwardly and waved hello. She was beautiful, and she was fast approaching. I had to think fast, so I shifted my right heel forward and tried to appear sexy. What that movement did was entirely subjective. To me, that movement was powerful. She noticed.

"Really?"

"What?"

"I saw you do that.'"

"Do what?"

"Shift your heel forward to place your very sharp, very sexy hip forward so you could show me your paraphernalia. I'm Sonja, by the way."

I think I'm in love.

"Oh, that, I was just...oh, never mind. You caught me."

Sonja now stood directly across from me, and I stared. I wasn't sure what to say.

"So are you going to tell me your name?"

Oh my god, I had forgotten entirely about my name. I had to regroup for a millisecond because my inner devil was still drooling over this gorgeous and intelligent woman.

"Oh, I'm sorry. I'm Melanie."

Oh god, I'm terrible at this. What the hell was I thinking, trying to get this girl's attention? She's reaching out, like right now. Oh my god, she's touching my hand now. My hand is approaching her lips. She's kissing it.

"Enchanted, Melanie."

"Oh, you as well, I guess?"

She knew I was very awkward, but I think she liked it. The conversation began when she mentioned my dress, and we started talking. Work never entered the discord, thank God. The night went on, and I didn't even notice the room filling with more people. It was 11:30 p.m. I guess Parisians party late.

Sonja and I sat on that corner and chuckled, and we began to posture ourselves against each other. I think it was the sexual tension building. Anyways, the clock struck midnight, and the door swung way wide open. I couldn't believe my eyes; it was a sea of prostitutes flooding into the room. My eyes sprung free from my slightly drunk facial expression, and I was *shocked*. Sonja was not. A swarm of absurdly beautiful women had come bursting into this party, and everyone was casual about it.

I felt sick. I deduced that I had too much to drink. Then my mind began to wander more, and I questioned, *Where was I?* I needed to use the restroom suddenly. I apologized to Sonja, and I quickly took off to the nearest washroom. Well, first, I had to get through this onslaught of beautiful Frenchwomen. As I pushed my way through the waves of women, I began to spin. The world was disconnecting itself from my head, and I was wondering if Sonja had drugged me.

No, that couldn't be. I had my drink in my hand the whole time. I even went to the bar to get it myself. *Focus. Find the washroom and recollect.* Finally, after swimming through a sea of skin and lingerie, I had found the restroom. I breached into it like a SWAT team during a drug bust. I quickly hauled myself toward the toilet, and I tried to hurl. Nothing. Nothing came out.

The world quickly stopped spinning, and I was utterly confused. Did I just have a panic attack? *Now* I didn't feel sick at all. *Okay, settle down. Let me look in the mirror.* My reflection stared back at me, and I recognized her. *Okay, so I'm not drugged. I'm slightly drunk. That's a plus.* I splashed some water on my face, and I grabbed those soft towels my boss had left out. Then I looked in the mirror one more time, just to be sure.

Everything appeared okay, so I exited the washroom. And there he was. Pierre, my boss, was wearing a Venetian Carnival mask, a dashing tuxedo top, and no pants or underwear. Hanging in between was a very large, um… Give me a moment. I'm still…uh…never mind.

Don't think about it.
Don't think about it.
Don't—

"Melanie, right? You got the note. You read the note. You came. Well, I'm not sure if you came yet, but we can fix that."

"Hi, Pierre. So I'm going to ignore the"—I coughed—"the elephant in the room and just imagine you with pants on while we're having this discussion."

"Melanie, do you not like? I am panting less for you, no? My note, uh, it was an invite for sex."

"Oh. Pierre, I'm terribly sorry, but I thought this was just like a *work party*, and then I saw the strippers…wait, sorry, prostitutes. Then I see this. I mean, it's wonderful. Do not let anyone tell you different, but I think I better go."

Then it was silence. The very awkward stares raged on. Then I finally spoke, "I'm going to go out for a cigarette."

I might have shouldered my well-equipped boss on the way out, and I continued toward the door. As I grabbed the handle, the door swung open, and another surprise awaited me. Standing directly outside Pierre's entry was a leather-clad dominatrix and a very scary-looking Siberian tiger on a chain. This could not get any weirder. Seriously.

"Bonsoir, Je crois que—"

"I'm terribly sorry, but English?"

"Ah, Americain. I'm here for the party, darling."

"I figured. It's not my party, so I'm just going to let you in."

"I would sincerely hope so, darling. Too bad you're leaving. You look like you taste good."

My face scrounged, and I darted for the elevator. The tiger growled, but the dom didn't let it growl again. The trick? A leather whip to master its startling movement.

As I waited for the elevator, I tapped, and my mind raced. What was I experiencing?

I really needed that cigarette.

The elevator dinged, and I hopped in. Seconds passed. Well, I didn't really know how long, but that was what it felt like. Dropping in seconds. The elevator. Whoa. As I reached the ground floor, I moved toward the door and prayed another tiger would not appear behind it.

Oh, thank God there wasn't. A sigh of relief escaped me, and I struggled to find the pack of Camel in my purse. My hands shakingly grabbed them, and I flicked my lighter so fast that the black putrid and oh-so-delicious smoke ignited and plastered itself into my lungs. Heavenly—the only way to describe it.

As I puffed and inhaled, I started to look around. It was my first Saturday night in Paris, and it was off to a roaring start. Company orgies, prostitutes, masks, leather, and even a *tiger*. Yes, it was quite the roaring start. Anyways, I was looking at the streets laid before me, and it seemed I had a choice to make. There was a fork on this road, and I could go either left or right. Today felt like a left kind of day, so I took a left. I figured tonight couldn't get any weirder, so I began walking. The cigarette quickly disintegrated in my shaky hands, and I wished I had brought a jacket. It was now 1:15 a.m. The noise from the streets was still exceptionally busy. As I exited onto the main road, lights bombarded the hazy mists pouring from the sidewalk, and I felt like Marilyn.

Except my dress never flew up. Instead, I just saw the pile of cigarette butts lying in the gutter and tossed my own into it. Might as well make my mark now. So I assumed I was in the Sixth Arrondissement based on the signage from the city markers. The green block read Les Boulevard Saint-Germain. It sounded familiar in my head, so I kept on heading down it. The night was beautiful, and the air felt clean. Cars grazed by, but there wasn't any honking. Not like New York, at least. The little cafés and stores along the way looked amazing, and the night's earlier festivities almost began disappearing from my memory. That was until I felt a tap on my shoulder. I quickly turned around, and there she was. Sonja had followed me out of the party. She must have seen my incident with Pierre.

"Hi. You ran off without saying goodbye. I hope you are all right."

"Oh, thanks. Yeah, I didn't feel so good. I think I needed the night air."

"What are you doing right now? I know a place. We can go there."

"Are...are you asking me to go to your place?"

"Oh, non. Jusque un café, ma chérie."

I was so relieved. A proper date.

"*Un café*, that's coffee, right?"

"Oui, my little one. Come follow me."

She grabbed my hand, and we began walking down the street. It was warm. She was…she was almost everything I imagined Paris to be. She was glowing, smart, sexy, and just everything and every emotion at once. Sonja…

We halted and turned left down to a red-lighted sign. It read Café. She squeezed my hand, and she looked at me. She asked me to wait for a couple of minutes while she ran in to see if it was okay for the two of us to drink coffee outside. I let her hand go, and the thought to have another cigarette appeared in my head.

I lit up, and I waited. A minute passed, and there was Sonja, right on time. She had two *cafés* in her hand, and she sat down at the cute, little table under the red neon. I sucked like hell and threw whatever wasn't used to the street. I took a seat next to her, and she grabbed my hand again.

"Melanie, I know we just met, but may I kiss you?"

I blushed. I leaned in. It happened. Wow.

"That…"

"My place?"

I replied with the only French I really knew, "Oui."

She dropped two euros on the table, gripped my hand tight, and pulled me up. Sonja told me her flat was only a block away, and we hurried there. We stopped to kiss a few more times in between. I couldn't help myself. It was this attraction. We reached her building's doorstep, and she was giggling. I reached into my purse to pull that old crumpling bag of cigarettes one more time for the night, and Sonja grabbed my hand.

"Upstairs. You can wait. I'll let you have one of mine after."

"After what?"

"After I go down on you."

I pressed my hand against the door to open it as fast as possible. Sonja pressed the button on the dial as we were pressing against each other's face with our tongues. That familiar ding struck, and we practically stumbled into the metal cage. The second ding struck, and we stumbled out one more time. She rummaged through her purse without taking her eyes off me, and she found the keys to her place. She inserted them, and she looked at me while doing so. Her tongue was moving in a manner that was so provocative that I'm hesitant to describe it here.

The door opened, and I saw her fling her bag onto the couch. She motioned her fingers for me to come inside, and I did. I stepped inside, and the lights still weren't on. It was okay. It was always better when they were off anyways.

She reached for my hand one more time, and I grabbed it. Out of the corner of my eye, I saw a shadow move from behind one of her drapes. It quickly approached and struck Sonja's head without thought. Before I could let out even a squeal, I felt blood rush to my head, and it all went *black*.

People describe the taste of blood as copper mostly, but tonight, I tasted a hint of tin. Don't ask me how I know the difference, but I do. That was my lip bleeding by the way. The room was still dark, but I could see glimpses of the horizon drawing out across the closed drapes. My hands were tied behind my back. Everything hurt. My legs were tied up as well. This chair felt old, but... I then felt the skin behind me. I hope it was Sonja. I began thinking, and I tried to wriggle my toes. *Okay, that's good. My senses are reconnecting. I don't know where the assailants are, or that's what I assume they are. I hope they won't torture us. Please just let it be a house robber. Please.*

Then I heard it. It was this noise, like *tick, titch, tick, titch, tick.*

Someone was either approaching or watching. It was just too dark for my eyes to see. My heart was racing, but I couldn't feel the pounding. It was this fusion of adrenaline and overwhelming fear that was feeding my drive to stay awake. *Stay awake. I must stay awake. I think if I can nudge my chair and wriggle Sonja and I loose, then...*

Clap. Clap. Clap.

"Well, well, well. Melanie Percourt. It's been too long, sweetie. You never even told me you were running off to Paris. Was New York not good enough for you? Did you even think about me while you were wandering the streets of Paris?"

ANTHOLOGY

No, no fucking way. Absolutely, no fucking way. There is no way in Sam Hill this bastard knows I'm here.

"Donny...I don't know how you got here or found out where I was...but, Donny, I need you to listen to me. You have to let me go. You have to give my friend leave as well, okay? We can take this somewhere else...just not here. Please."

I smelled those old cigars he would always smoke back in New York. Donny was complicated. He and I were together for some time. I thought we were going to get hitched a few years ago, but things changed. He moved into my line of sight. He looked the same—the same strange scar down his left eye, the same posture that took me off my feet, and those bright baby-blue eyes, the eyes of a scoundrel-to-be.

"Melanie, I don't think you have much of a say here, darlin'. You see, I have answers to the questions pouring out of your stupid hole from a few seconds ago. You see, I don't want to be the asshole who never explains how he never found you."

"Donny, please."

"Melanie, SHUT THE FUCK UP! You don't get to speak."

I was sweating, and the ties around my feet and legs were steeping in the brewing sweat. I was scared now. Donny, my schizophrenic, drug-abusing, asshole of an ex, was here about to do God knows what to Sonja and me. Then I heard another voice enter the fray.

"Take a step back now, boy."

There was another voice—dark, deep, creamy. I think the stranger was black. Then I felt touch. It was cold. It felt almost *cruel*. He made his way around to my line of sight, and he was tall. Not just tall but *tall*. His accent, I would guess African, but I didn't want to guess wrong. I think I'm just going to listen now.

"Melanie Percourt graduated Princeton with a master's in English literature and communications. Lost her mother at ten from a drunk-driving incident. Lost her father at twelve to a suicide. Grew up in Brooklyn Orphanage. Taken in by the Devorahs. Then sent to school abroad—England, finishing school. She graduated and returned to the city that birthed her. Now after four years at your firm, you have achieved this promotion and moved once again. Now it's Paris. Where to next, little one?"

He knew everything about me, and for some reason, that didn't seem scary. You could practically decipher all that about me from the Internet. I was more scared of Donny than him right now. This tall man was the only thing holding Donny back.

Okay, let's see if he would listen.

"Thank you for reading my life story back to me, but will you please let the woman behind me go. If this is a revenge deal or the normal ex-boyfriend jealousy, then she shouldn't be a victim. I know you're a good person deep down, and you don't want to harm this woman."

He stared soullessly. His eyes were melting into my skull. The visions were… I felt like sleeping suddenly. Did he inject me with something? Suddenly, the edges began filling in, and I was helpless. *What did I say? Oh no. Open. Open. Please…*

It was pitch-black.

I was alone. This place, it was neither cold nor warm. I couldn't feel the wind. I couldn't feel…

"To think that you're alone in here is very unwise, little one."

"Mister, please, I didn't do anything wrong. I just left, okay? I left New York because I was tired. I was stressed. I was only there because of him, and I felt like I had to be with him. He was…Donny was broken. I felt like I had to fix him. No one else could. So I put up with it. I put up with the nights he didn't remember hitting me or the nights he raped me, and I lay there because deep down, I just wanted to make him feel better. I…I had to leave. I had to just start somewhere no one knew me. Tonight, I thought I was back into the thing I thought I had escaped. I guess that was the panic attack talking. Then I met this girl, and she was everything that Donny was when it all started. Started so long ago now it seems…"

The entire time I was pleading to this soulless…this man, he approached without a sound. His hands held behind his back with strength and reserve. And then he had finally reached me just floating in this pool of…nowhere. He had contacted me in nowhere, and he looked. As I pleaded and poured my soul unto him, he just stared.

In his hand, he held a pendant. There was a decorated skull with a long silver chain. He moved it up to his lip, and he spoke, "Melanie, wake up."

Then I was back. I could see the lights pouring in from the curtains. I was lying in a bed; I was no longer tied up. I glanced around, and the room appeared…it appeared to look as it should be if Sonja and I…

Sonja, where was Sonja?

"Sonja!"

Suddenly, next to me, a rustling appeared, and I prepared for the worst.

"Yes, what is…whoa. *Vous-êtes bien, Mélanie?*"

Oh my god, what was that?

"Sonja! Oh, I'm sorry. Umm, do you remember much from last night?"

"Oui, mi amor."

"Oh…" I was utterly confused. "What do you remember exactly?"

So she began explaining, and everything appeared perfect. Perfect, as in once we got back to her place, we made love all night and woke up with a bit of a hangover. No assailants, no questioning, just nothing. What was wrong with me?

We took it slow. She mounted me. She looked compassionately down at me, and she began to touch. I…

"Melanie, are you sure?"

Yes, I needed this. I needed this release. It was the stress. It'd been building since I left New York. That was just a dream. There was nothing to be worried about. So I pulled her waist to mine, and the morning went by. It was Sunday. We didn't need to do anything but lie here.

It was 5:00 p.m. We were still in bed. Sonja made coffee and ran to the boulangerie and brought us some great food. I was still shaking up from last night's dreams. What did I experience? I mean, it was so real.

Sonja entered back into her bedroom, and she told me that she had work in an hour.

"It's okay, Sonja. I'll be fine. Can…can I see you later?"

"*Oui, ma cher.* I would love to see you tonight. I'm off at midnight."

"Okay, I'll shoot you my address."

"*Parfait.*"

Sonja jumped onto the bed and kissed me goodbye. That was my queue to go scavenge whatever was left of my Sunday evening. I gathered my stuff, and it smelled like her. No blood either. Whew. I blew Sonja a kiss goodbye, and I left.

Out on the street, I reached into my bag to grab those old Camels, and I felt something that shouldn't be in my pocket. I pulled it out, and there it was…another note. Listed was an address. Nothing else. How did this get in here? Did Sonja put it here? Well, I could look up the address on my phone, so that was what I did. Apparently, it was a building near Les Champs-Élysées. Hell, I had a few hours before Sonja came over, and she'd already seen me at my worst, so I might as well explore this note.

I was on the metro, but I didn't remember walking down into the subway. There was music playing in my ears, but I didn't have earbuds in. Also, I was the only one in the metro.

"Hello?"

No response, just this music and the train tracks.

Am I going insane?

The metro reached my stop, and I exited. No one, absolutely no one, was in the metro. *Is there some national holiday or something? Okay, let me just get to this address and see what the hell is going on.* As I walked out of the underground, I noticed everyone was wearing the same type of mask from my boss's party last night. Was there a carnival in Paris? As I began walking, the map on my telephone alerted me to go five hundred feet northbound, and I should reach my destination. I made a 180-degree turn, and I saw the building number. I walked toward it, and in the doorway, there was a man.

"Hello, Melanie. I hope you found my note. Tell me, did you experience strange occurring last night?"

I didn't want to answer. I just wanted to turn around before another nightmare unleashed itself unto me. But I couldn't turn around; I was compelled to listen.

"Melanie, my name is Mr. Jacket. I am an acquaintance of your ex-boyfriend, Donny Blaze. He wanted to see where you ran off to. Now, Ms. Percourt, I normally do not take cases like yours, but…"

"I'm sorry, did you say 'cases'?"

"Yes, my dear. Please allow me to explain."

He clicked his fingers. Again, the world faded along the edges, forming into cascading black waves. I was in nowhere again. This time, I sat at a table. There was a chessboard on the table, and the figurines were designed to look like people in my life. I wanted to scream, but I was compelled not to. Then I heard his voice once again.

"You have been marked, my dear. I am here to collect. You escaped. Plain and simple. You escaped when you shouldn't have. You thought you could leave your old life behind, but you must have forgotten about the night you originally met me? I assume that's why the days have been so foggy since I have returned to collect."

I couldn't speak. My mouth opened, but my voice sent no sound forward. The thoughts in my head were nil. I was listening, but I didn't want to hear.

"Would you care for me to refresh your memory?"

I couldn't speak.

"Very well then."

This felt like a dream, but I knew it was a memory, and I was living it again. Donny and I were in Grand Central Park. He was holding my hand, and I was bundled up from the cold. He was the opposite; his hand was running solely with heat. It was sweltering, but I wouldn't let go. He was all I have. As the freezing chill blasted against our faces, I remember us sitting down on a bench overlooking the little lake. The water was frozen over, and birds were playing on the twigs that were frozen facing upward. My hand was still touching Donny's, and I could see him reaching into his pocket. This was the moment. He was pulling out one of his needles and that cursed little bag out from his jacket pocket. *He's going to shoot up.* I decided that I needed to tell him to stop. I moved my other hand over the bag and needle and told him, "Another time, hon. Not here, please." He nodded. He put the bag back into his jacket, and we got up. Time then froze. I was back at the lake. Donny's gone, and I was alone.

Mr. Jacket appeared on the icy lake. He was just standing there…soullessly.

"I'm giving you a choice, Melanie. This was the moment. Memory moves in many absurd ways. In one, you never halted Donny from shooting up. He coerced you into taking some just to please him, and you stuck the needle through. Unfortunately, the dose Donny picked up earlier had been laced with rat poison. You two were strung and broken, your life dwindling on edge in Grand Central among the frozen and forgotten things. This memory you just experienced, this is how you wished it would've happened. Donny died that day. That was no mistake. He overdosed right next to you. A bad batch. The wrong tincture. You left yourself there in the city, and you haven't looked back since. You left yourself in the cold, despite you waking. Isn't that why you left in such a hurry? You felt as if you outran something you weren't supposed to. The promotion at random? Pack up and go? Tsk, tsk, tsk. My poor girl, you truly don't remember."

I was helpless. This memory had turned into a nightmare, and it was slowly coming back to me. Wait, the stranger said he was giving me a choice. Thoughts began returning into my psyche, and I could speak again.

"You said there's a choice… What is it?"

He stood there, and he formed a menacing grin. His body was gliding closer and closer to me as I stood, knowing I couldn't escape this. He was now in front of me, looking down, and he lifted his finger to his lips.

"Wake up, Melanie."

The edges began coming back, and color flooded in. I was back in Paris. I was in my flat. I was sitting with a cup of coffee. The bowl, it was chilling to the touch. How did I get here? Then I heard that all-too-familiar sound.

Tick, titch, tick, titch.

He came from the kitchen corner, and Sonja was in front of him. I spotted a sharp object steered toward her back.

"This is the choice, Melanie. I'm collecting on a debt owed today. It's going to be your life or hers. She will never remember any of this if you choose yourself. If not, then she dies, alone and cold with a needle in her arm, just like Donny."

"I don't understand… Why are you doing this to me? I never did anything wrong."

"No, no, no. Melanie. Can't you see? You did. You left. You left yourself on the bench. You left everything behind because you thought you could escape. There is no escape for you, dear. The past has come to collect. Think, why have I shown you all these things? Just think for one clear moment…"

A wave of memories came flooding back into my mind, and now I saw what I did. That day on the bench, I never told Donny to put the bag away. He and I both shot up on that bench. He died, and I survived. I should've never survived. So the reaper was here to collect. Now I know. I guess I lived past my time. I looked to the soulless man, and I understood. It'd all been a dream, except I lived it as a death wish. I was never in Paris; I was merely a ghost roaming long streets. I was never here because I was still in New York. I died on the park bench in New York. Now I'm in hell. A prolonged stay. Now I'm given an ultimatum.

"Take me. I know I've done wrong. I left selfishly. Let Sonja go, and you can have me."

They stood there. Less pressure was applied on the knife to Sonja's back.

"What's the difference between a dream and a nightmare, Melanie?" the soulless man asked.

"I…I'm not sure. I think a dream is how you wish the world to be, and a nightmare is how the world really is. Heh. So this is—"

"No, it's not that or the other. Melanie, look at me. Say goodbye to Sonja. Then you and I are going to go for a walk."

"Okay."

I walked up to them as he let the blade go from his hand. Sonja unfroze from his grip and rushed to me. No words needed to be spoken, and I kissed her with what was left of me. She gave me the same look she did at the party last night. I hope I'd always remember that.

"Good night, Sonja."

I followed Mr. Jacket out through the door, and it was white. I didn't know what was beyond, but I'd always remember the extra time I had here.

"Good night, world."

Fin

Chapter 2

On the Run

There was so much blood. I...

It was everywhere. I mean, my vision was practically going red from how much blood there was. Fuck, this was such a stupid, goddamn idea. What the hell were we thinking robbing a bank? *Fuck. Fuck. Fuck. Okay, try and keep a cool head. Turn on the AC, play the Zeppelin tape, and kick back. Forget that you have three dead partners in the car with you, forget about the blood spattered everywhere, forget about the blood and possibly bone of your best friend's skull on your cheek.*

"Ahhhhhhhhhhhhhhhhhhhhhhhhhhhhhhhhhh!"

Huff, huff. Okay, it was dark. I just needed to keep driving. I needed to get out of Nebraska, cross the state line, ditch the car on the road, walk to a motel, keep it low-key for a day, hot-wire another ride, and pass a few more state lines. Then it would be good to lie low for a while.

Okay...okay, that's the plan. Just keep driving, and I'll get there. Just keep driving. Don't think about it. Don't think about Billy, John, and Mark. They're dead. No point to ponder on the deceased.

It was silent for a hundred miles. Nothing but plains of nothing. My headlights, the road, no radio, just silence. The tires grazing across the asphalt barely made a noise. It was the rotation that was almost relaxing me, but I thought my ears might be blown out from the gunshots when it all went wrong. My stomach began to growl. I was sure the adrenaline ate up all the energy that I had stored away. *Good thing I ate those frosted flakes forty minutes before the gig.* I was tired and hungry. I'd need to pull over soon. I prayed there was a diner or motel or just something along the highway.

There was silence and wind—the howling winds. Two-lane highway and me, alone.

Another thirty minutes went by. I stopped keeping count of the miles. My eyes were slowly closing. I thought I saw a light on the horizon. I checked the time, and it should be dark for another couple of hours. I prayed it was a diner. I could park, eat a burger, and get some coffee. Just…I just needed something. The growling hurt now; my head was pounding.

Okay, here we go over the crest. Thank God we're over it now.

There it was in all its beauty—the diner in the middle of nowhere. I finally stepped on the brakes, friendly and easy, so I wouldn't look suspicious rolling in. I saw the lights on, so that must mean they were open. I rolled up real slow, and I turned off the lights. I had shades to cover the windows in the glove, so I placed those all around. *I hope there aren't any bullet holes in the car.* I couldn't tell you how many shots I heard fired once we got going. Finally, after padding up the car, I stepped out and saw the neon shining down on me.

"Diner, 24-7."

Under the neon blues, I walked into a happy place. I saw a gentleman sitting in the far-left corner. He was wearing a large white trench coat and seemed to be reading the paper. His car must be in the back. I thought I didn't see it out front. I rang the bell on the counter, and he didn't even pull the paper down. A noise from the kitchen rattled through the empty zone.

"One minute!"

Oh, thank God.

"Yeah, yeah…take your time. I'll take a seat."

I seated myself on the far-right side of the diner and grabbed one of the day's papers along the bar. I thought this would be the first time I ever read the article. As soon as I took my seat, a gorgeous, small-town blondie came from the kitchen in her cute apron and hair tie. She had the smile of an angel, and it calmed me down…for even just a little.

"What will it be, hon?"

"Oh…sorry. I'll take a coffee and a burger, please. No cheese."

"Great, will that be all?"

"I believe so. Say, what brings a pretty girl like you all the way out here?"

"Fella, I…I don't mean to be rude, but let's just stick to the customer-employee thing."

"Oh, sorry."

"I'll have your order right up."

"Thanks."

Well, that was embarrassing. Nothing was going right today. I slouched back into the squeaky plastic bar seats. As I rolled into the most comfortable position I could think of, my eyes darted to the opposite side of the diner. The strange fellow was no longer there, just a coffee cup.

"Norman."

I looked to my right, and behind the counter was the man I saw when I walked in. How did I not see him move? I wondered if he worked here.

"Do I know you?"

"No, kid, I don't believe you do."

"So do you work here or something'?"

"I reckon I don't."

"Behind the counter, then just for the hell of it?"

"If it pleases me, then yes."

"Would the waitress approve?"

"Oh, I wouldn't worry about her. It seems to be just you and me, Norman."

Okay, the hair on the back of my neck was raising directly toward the heavens. Here I was fresh off a bank robbery, on the run from state police, with three dead friends in the car, and I was seated inside a diner talking to a man who knew my name, yet I'd never met him before. The waitress! I could ask her to come on out.

"Hello! Waitress! Can I make a change to my order?"

"Son, she's out back on her smoke break. She won't hear you. May I take a seat with you?"

"Depends, tell me how you know my name."

As he moved from behind the counter, I could now see his entire frame. He was massive.

"I know quite a few names, Norman. Are you asking how I know yours specifically?"

"Yes."

He took a seat directly across the table, staring—that was what he was doing—in absolute silence. His eyes…I'd never seen anything like them before. They were soulless things. I couldn't decide whether I should be afraid or intrigued.

"Well, Norman, I know why you're here."

"A-and why's that, mister?"

"Jacket. Mr. Jacket. Why you ask, son? Well, I know you're on the run…"

Fuck. How could he know? I… There must be a spot of blood somewhere on me. I had a guilty face riddled all over my expression, and now I was sweating. He was just going to keep drilling me.

"Are you okay, Norman? You seem to be uncomfortable. Am I making you uncomfortable?"

"N-n-no, sir, it's just…"

Then it clicked in my head. *Just lie. He doesn't know.*

"Well, I've been on the run for a while, you see. My ma and pa, they kicked me out for roughing around in the household. Ya know, with a girl they didn't take a liking to. She and I split up a few hundred miles back after an argument, and now it's just me."

"That's a lie."

He knows. He knows. He knows.

"Say, Norman, how about I go out for a cigarette. When I come back, I hope you can tell me the truth."

The tall man hovered over the table as he stood up. He grabbed a pristine pack of unlabeled cigarettes from his jacket pocket and lit one up. In his eyes, a flicker of a shining star struck my soul to the core. I was paralyzed in my seat. I was helpless to him walking away for a smoke break. As I saw him walk out the diner door, I heard two simultaneous rings.

"Sorry, hon. I took a quick break out back. The coffee and burger will be right up."

I almost forgot why I was here. *All right, Norman, keep your head on a swivel. Eat the grub, then get the fuck out of here before any more questioning.* Thank God, I saw her coming out from the kitchen with a plate and a cup.

"Care for any room in your cup?"

"No. Black, please."

She set down the order, and instantly I began eating. I forgot how hungry I was. My stomach was practically running inside out at this point.

"Well, I guess one of us is starving."

I looked up, and she still had that cute, little grin on her face. She was the sole person to make this day any more comforting.

"May I ask you something?"

"Sure, hon."

"That man who was sitting in that booth back there, what time did he come in?"

She looked at me, perplexed of my question.

"Ah, I'm sorry, but you've been the only customer I've had in a few hours. No one has been here since you got here."

"No, no, no, that's not right. A substantial tall gentleman in a large white trench coat, he was sitting right there in that booth when I walked in. For God's sake, there's even a coffee cup where he was sitting."

"I'm sorry, but that's my cup."

We stared at each other, searching each other's expression for an answer. Neither of us reached an understanding.

"It sounds like you have a lot on your mind. I'll leave you to your food. Ring the bell if you need anything. I'll be in the back."

I needed to go outside. I needed to see if the gentleman was there.

"Do you have a cigarette? I...I could really use one right now."

"Sure, hon."

She reached into her apron and pulled out her American Spirit and handed me the minted little cylinder.

"Thanks."

I left everything on the table, and she offered a light. I took it and quickly dashed to get out. As I pushed open the door, I didn't see any white trench coat smoking outside. Where could the enormous man have gone? As I took a quick rip of the tiny piece of calming, I noticed lights along the horizon. Fortunately, I still had a few more hours of nightfall, so I knew it must be a passing car. As the lights slowly crawled over the hill, I noticed it began to slow down. I thought he was going to pull into the diner. *Shit. I don't need more people showing up. I have three bodies in my car and a few million in duffels.*

The car slowly rolled up, and I took one last rip before I saw the side of the vehicle. It read State Police Highway Patrol. *I am so fucked.* I flicked the cigarette onto the pile already next to the door, and I headed back in. I needed to get out of here quick.

I returned to my booth, and the food and coffee were still steaming. Thank God, I needed a warm fucking meal. It was too cold out. This whole night had been too cold. I started scarfing down the food when I heard the diner door fully open. That little jingle of the bell. The voice of the waitress. The sound of boot heels clicking on the plated floor.

"Be right out!"

"Take your time, Val."

The officer now looked around the diner and looked at me. He gave me a quick nod and took a seat at the restaurant. He must be a regular; he obviously knew the waitress. The waitress came out from behind the kitchen, and she went to take the officer's order. The words that came out of her mouth, well shit.

"Hey, darling. How's my baby girl doing tonight? No weirdos, I hope."

"None tonight, Daddy. Jus' that young fella in the corner. I think he might be a little stressed from the cold."

I kept my head down, pretending not to listen in on their conversation.

"Hey, son. The weather got you a bit shaking tonight?"

I kept my head down, scarfing down the food. I needed to get out of here.

"Son?"

"S-sorry, Officer. I'm on a bit of a schedule, that's all. I gotta reach the farmhouse by dawn. Otherwise, my father will kill me."

"No shit, you have a place around here?"

"No…no, sir. Across the state line, sir. Pa had me running some errands with a partner of ours two lines over."

"Ah, I see. Taking a quick bite before heading back on the road. Say, what's got you shaking up? Your fork is practically a pendulum."

I hadn't even noticed that my fingers were shaking so hard. My entire body had been buzzing to the tone of this man's voice.

"A bit too much coffee, I think, sir."

"Heh. We all get there sometimes."

The officer and his daughter continued with their conversation. I tuned out. I had to be somewhere else; I didn't know where. Anywhere seemed better than here, really. I finished the burger, chugged the rest of the coffee, left the cash on the table, and dipped out before anyone could say anything.

"Thank you for the service."

I budged the door open and made a brisk walk to my car. As I peeked my head up, I noticed the man in the trench coat. He'd been out here all this time. He was just here, smoking his cigarette. I heard the diner's bell, and I turned around to see.

"Hon, do you need your change?"

"No, go ahead and keep it."

"Thank you. Good luck getting to where you're going."

"Thanks."

As I moved to turn back around, Mr. Jacket was now a mere five feet away.

"You ready to have that discussion now, Norman?"

"W-where did you go? I…you're not real."

He began to circle me, and I followed him.

"Son, I'm genuine. Ask me anything. I'll bet you I'll know the answer. Here's a question, Norman. What's in the car?"

No. I'm not going to answer that.

"Nothing."

"Really?"

He halted, his stance sideways. He turned his head, and his starry eyes cut through me.

"May I check myself? I know you're hiding, *Norman*. Just tell me the truth. That's all I ask."

I felt compelled. I wanted to tell him. *I...I... No, stop. Don't tell him.* But like a fish I grabbed in a pond, the truth just came out.

"It's Billy, John, and Mark!"

I dropped to my knees. The confession proved its weight—the burden of my friends' souls on my now grieving and guilty hear. I was helpless. *Take me*, I thought. *Whoever this man is, just...take me.* I looked up to see his reaction, but he was no longer there. I looked all around, and there were zero traces of anyone being here. I scanned the ground, and the dust had zero evidence of his heel tracks. I saw one pair, and they were mine. Did I just confess to midair? What was going on with me?

"I can't breathe. Ugh. Uck. Ack. I...I can't breathe."

I collapsed. I didn't feel anything, couldn't hear anything. I just felt the burden. It was anchoring itself onto my lungs. It was hard to breathe now, harder than it had ever been. As my eyes began to close, I saw legs approaching. I saw a mouth moving, but I couldn't quite make out wh—.

Ugh. What. Wh-where am I? I c-can't see. Wait, am I talking to myself?

"Norman?"

Beep. Beep. Beep. Beep. Beep. Beep. Beep. Beeeeeeep.

"Norman! Norman, you gotta wake up!"

As my eyes slowly began to open, the light pierced them, and I was blinded. I was lost. I didn't know anything. The question I wanted to ask, I'd most likely get the answer to in a second. It was coming back now. *Why-why am I thinking so clearly?* As I looked around, I saw that I was in a white room. It l-looked padded...heavily.

"Norman, son. You've been out for quite some time. I'm going to need you to listen to this. Don't wrestle against the restraints either, son. They're only to keep you from harming yourself. Norman, what do you remember? What do you remember before waking up just now?"

I wanted to speak, but my voice felt heavy. It was staying down in my throat. I wanted it to come out. I wanted to talk, and they were waiting. They were just staring...so soullessly. *No, it's him. It's them. No. No. No. Get me out of here. Please. No. He's...he's...!*

"Norman, calm down! You will only hurt yourself. Listen to us, Norman. Do you remember who we are?"

Finally, my voice returned.

"Mr. Jacket! Mr. Jacket! Get away. Get away!"

"Norman, who is Mr. Jacket? My name is Dr. Mark, and this is Nurse Billy. Dr. Valarie has been doing the rotations with me. You kept yelling our names in your sleep, son. You've been asleep for... well, it's been quite some time."

I looked to see this man move to open the windows to my room.

"What are you doing? Stop, please."

"Norman, I need you to see this. Hopefully, this will bring some memories back."

As he opened up the window, I saw an ocean of black—a starry abyss. *I...I'm in space.* I looked to the "doctors," and I felt scared. I...I didn't know whether to ask if all this was real or... *Oh god, I am insane. I've...space.*

"Doc, are...are we in space?"

He made a quick glance over to Dr. Valarie, who had just entered my room.

"Norman, please. Let me explain."

"Then explain, Doc! Can't you see I'm losing it here!"

I was practically pulling my eyes out. *Why won't anyone just give me a straight fucking answer!*

"Norman, you're on the United Continents Lunar Institute for the Mentally Ill (UCLIMI). You've been here since your *psychotic break* in July 2147. You murdered your two brothers at the age of ten without recollection of ever taking action. Your name was *Benjamin* before that incident. That break then formed two completely new rogue identities. You have chosen *Norman*, on most occasions, to remain in control as your primary personality. After years of observation here, we have discovered that you have DID, an extreme variation. Son, you have three distinct personalities who know nothing about one another. You are in this cell for one reason only. That reason is because of your third personality and most deadly identity. Think of him as the…well, the proverbial monster under the bed. The dark *id*. It calls itself *Mr. Jacket*, and Jacket is a relentless, merciless, manipulative, obsessed individual who will stop at nothing to slaughter any and everything around it. That's why you're here, Norman. It's for your protection and the protection of others. You went catatonic for quite some time. Almost twelve months. We believed it was your consciousness battling for control on the inside. We found high and extremely hyperdeveloped brain activity during your coma. This indicated intense and vivid dreaming. I'm truly sorry that after all this time, we haven't found any way to help, son. I really am."

Speechless, one could say I was. The funny thing? At that moment, it wasn't much of a surprise. I wasn't sweating. I wasn't scared. I actually laughed. After that, I was not really sure. My mind vibrated off sounds of screaming, and I felt warm liquid over my body. There were echoes of pleading, and I was watching it all happen. I was helpless to stop it. I saw lights blaring red, and my ears were ringing with sirens, but it was a distant echo. The door closed to my room, and it was painted freshly red, black, Caucasian, African, Asian, Native, and white. I walked to the window to see the big blue ball in the floating abyss, and I knew the reflection…

Starry black eyes. How beautiful.

"Thank you for finally letting me out, *Norman*."

Fin

Chapter 3

The *Trip* of a Lifetime

Leo, Michelle, Jessica, JJ, and I all decided that after the last lecture of the day, we would meet at Leo's house first to drop off all the cars. Then we would drive up to the mountain and go to that one camping spot we stopped at last year during our annual trip. This year, we decided to take another kind of trip. We were getting older; our minds were expanding. We conjured up the idea to bring some hallucinogens on our trip. I had this idea, that we all wanted to experience euphoria together. You know, best friends forever and all that bullshit. At least that was what the girls thought of it as. The boys and I really just wanted to trip. Now the only problem was securing the means of obtaining these drugs. Leo said he knew a guy off White Street, only a few blocks from the school, who was dealing some shit to his older brother at community college. I mean, why not, right? We were seniors; we could make our own drug deals.

We had two days before we were leaving. Leo and I had planned to go to White Street after our last lecture. At lunch, we invited JJ to come with us, but he and Jessica were off fucking or something. Michelle said she would be down only if she dreamed of being raped in a drug dealer's house for fun. Jeez. So there we were, the lone warriors charging onward to the realm of hallucinogens. Leo looked fearless; I knew he was chill about most "adult" situations. I could pretty much trust him with anything. Like that one time Leo covered up that…never mind.

On the roads through suburbia, I saw scattered houses. Most were being built up or renovated. The city must have something to do with that. Then we pulled to the stop, and right above us, it read in white print, White Street. We looked to our left, and there it was, our destination. Leo pulled up the car across the street. I looked at him, and we nodded. I packed my knife in my pocket, just in case.

"So your brother picks up from him. What for?"

"Oh, Jesse is microdosing. Apparently, it's supposed to help expand your mind or some shit like that. I think he just likes to get high."

"Says the kid buying some acid for us."

"Hey, we're buying this acid, Justin. Don't forget you're coming in with me."

As we approached the staircase leading up to the white doors, I could feel eyes peering down on us. I looked up, yet no one was there. That eerie and sudden chill that strikes your back, making you twitch freakishly, just occurred twice. It was unsettling, but I was not going to chicken out and leave Leo. Everything was going to be okay. Leo proceeded to knock on the door, and within a few seconds, it opened. A beautiful teenage girl with black hair, black skin, and brown eyes in a pretty sunflower dress greeted us.

"Leo, Justin, the mister, was expecting you. Come. Come."

She began rapidly moving her hand to wave us in. She was acting like my grandmother, and she looked the same age as us. I couldn't tell whether my fear scale should jump a notch or my pity scale should jump two. Leo walked in without a care, and I followed close in pursuit. As she guided us to the middle room on the right-hand side of the house, I caught a peek of a collection of swords. Not just swords for sword's sake but *swords*. Okay, I'm like a complete and total weaponry nerd. I just love looking, waving, weighing, and pointing guns, swords, knives, daggers, katanas, cutlass, Viking weapons, scimitars, LMGs, oh, and most of all, explosives. I'm not like a sociopath or anything though. I don't let that little voice take control. I'd been helped with that already.

So we entered into this parlor room, and the fireplace was exuding a sweltering wave of death presented by heat. I was amazed of the fact that nothing had melted or caught fire to any and all present. Even the little odd maid, whose name I forgot to ask for. But as she motioned to move me closer to the surface of the sun, I hesitantly stepped and saw an even more immense array of weaponry. I was astonished. Leo had already gone to Mr. Jacket. He was actually at his side, and Jacket seemed to be whispering something in his ear.

"Are you going to introduce me, Leo?"

"W—oh, yeah. Mr. Jacket, this is Justin. He…he's a friend of mine."

I saw Leo move his hand to scratch his words with shame. That gnawing itch at the back of his skull. Me? I was fuming, but you really couldn't tell from the sweltering heat. As I was about to speak my mind, the very tall petticoated man stood from his chair and turned his head toward me. Suddenly, my eyes fell to him, for a starry abyss was all I saw. It was all I knew.

"Hello, Justin, I'm going to need you to sleep now. Everything will be all right. Leo and I need to have a little chat. Rest well."

As the stars continued to flood into the corners and peeled back years of my reality, I dropped into a void. Everything just went *click*, like a light switch.

The next thing I knew, I was back in the car. But, it was not Leo's car. We were in Michelle's car. I looked out the window, still in a drugged state, and I saw woods, trees, pines, and snow. We were already on our way up the mountain for the weekend. That was why we were in Michelle's because she had an SUV. Fuck, my head really hurt. It was like everything was just turning back online. All the switches were being flicked one by one. I was in the back seat, Michelle and Leo were up front, while Jessica and JJ were cuddling to the left of me, asleep. How long was I out? What happened in that house? Mister…his eyes. I must've passed out from not eating enough that day or something. Low on water. As soon as I got my voice reactivated, I'd—

"Holy shit, Leo! Look out!"

As I saw three prancing deer nearly deck the hood of our car, I saw Leo's instinctual turn of the wheel, and the swerve commenced. The vehicle rapidly and violently whipped out of control. The roads must still be cold; the sun was barely coming up. *Why am I so calm? This may be the end, and I'm missing so much time...*

The headlights peered over the edge, and we saw a wall of rock and snow. Leo strangled the wheel, and I heard the brakes screech and squeal as the tires underneath reared and gripped for control. Then it was quiet. We were okay. No one appeared hurt. The car, I think, just tapped the tip of the rock. Michelle was breathing painfully, but I think it was just her asthma. She reached to grab her inhaler. Jessica and JJ were still tangled together, now even more so. Me? I was locked in my seat belt, completely normal, unharmed and surprisingly unafraid. I think it was because everything just seemed to flick a switch. It would now be a proper time to ask why the hell I'd been passed out for so long, but everyone thought it was somehow normal.

"I need to check outside, Miche. Oh, good, the sleeping prince finally wakes. Justin, come out of the car and help me look around. Make sure we didn't hit anything or damage some shit."

He looked at me for an answer, but my blank expression stated everything. To him, it was like nothing ever happened.

"Yeah. Sure. I'll do that."

I saw my jacket bundled on the floor between Michelle's seat and mine, and I reached down for it as I heard Michelle take her second albuterol pill. After I grabbed my jacket and put it on, I tugged on the door handle, and I was embraced by a freezing chill. We were definitely on the mountain, and I fully realized it then.

"Hey, Justin. I know you probably have a lot of questions. Don't get pissed, all right?"

He spoke before I even saw him around the corner. It was like he knew I wanted to punch the shit out of his face. So I took that sharp turn and looked directly at him.

"You're right. I do have a ton of questions, but first…"

Fuck it. I decked him in his nose. Friends don't do that shit to other friends, especially not ones like Leo and me.

"Fuck…okay, I deserved that. We're good, Justin. We're good."

"We damn well better be good. I want to know everything that's happened since we were on White Street. Everything. It's like there was a switch in my brain, and I fell asleep and then woke up here."

"Got a good left throw there, buddy. All right, so this is going to be hard to explain, but you really have been asleep for a day. Well, almost a day. It's the early morning because we left last night. Figured we would spend a day to relax and get all the gear set up. And since you were KO'd for God knows how long, we kind of made the decisions with everyone awake. I just told everyone you had a bad trip on one of the heavier mushrooms we picked up at Mr. Jacket's."

There was no way he just came up with that on the spot. He'd been plotting to say that in his head. Mr. Jacket, that guy must've screwed with both of our heads. That was why everything is just in the wrong place.

"Tell me about Mr. Jacket, Leo. What did he whisper to you before I was knocked unconscious? He didn't even lay a hand on me, and I hit the deck like a stone. I just vaguely remember him talking to you before and after. Just tell me, man."

"All right. All right. I didn't want you or the others to find out, but I wanted to try some DMT. My brother told me he had a killer batch, and I wanted to keep it quiet, considering we all decided to just do shrooms. Justin, I just wanted to trip without being judged."

"Bullshit, Leo!"

I heard the car door open with aggressive strength.

"Hey, what's going on out here? We're literally in the middle of the fucking road, on a mountain highway. It's snowing, and I'm freezing. Let's go!"

That was Michelle. She was pissed that Leo was taking too long. I was just pissed in general.

"Justin, we'll talk later."

"Fine."

I didn't bother to check around the car. I just went back to my seat. The door's handle creaked, and I budged it open. Metal and cold, not the best combo. As I returned to my position, I saw that Jess and JJ were lighting up on some weed they grew at their place. They said it kept them warm.

"JJ, do you mind if I? I gotta blow off some steam. Gotta relax."

"Yeah! Yeah! Justin, take a rip of her, buddy."

I wasn't going to get any answers for the remainder of the ride, especially with the tension Michelle and I were putting on Leo. It pushed us all to a quiet drive up the rest of the mountain. I took a large toke from JJ's bong, and that put me on my ass. I just stared off into the scenery, blanked. Just how I wanted.

An hour passed by, and we decided to stop at the gas station for a fill-up. My stoned ass that could barely walk decided to go inside the store and get some treats. As I exited the car, I began walking toward the store when I saw Leo glance at me. His apologetic expression seemed sincere, but still, I needed answers. Forgiveness wasn't going to come until I had them. There was a flight of steps approaching, and I staggered up to them. Finally, I made it in, and I was in the chocolate factory. I grabbed a gallon of water, some Doritos, and a Coke Zero—the perfect balance of not overeating while under the influence. I got to the counter and placed a ten on it. The employee knew I was stoned, and he gave me my change with a jealous smile.

"I'd rather be where you are right now, my dude."

"Ha. I don't even know where I am right now."

I grabbed my nutrition, and I stumbled out the door back to the car. Within the ten-foot distance between the vehicle and the door, I saw a figure across the street. He was tall, and he was wearing white. The brim of his hat began to tilt up. My heart jumped from my chest. I bowed my head down, and I dashed to the car. It couldn't be him. I couldn't go through that again. I grabbed the car door, and my Coke dropped, spraying all over the ground. I didn't care. Everyone was already in the car. I looked to Leo with a grave expression.

"Let's go."

He knew something was wrong and simply nodded. That earned him a positive check on the forgiveness list. I kept my head down in the car, and I dared not look across the street. We rolled out of the gas station, and we were back on the road. The stop seemed to clear the air a little, and we only had twenty more minutes before we reached the campsite. JJ sparked the conversation, and finally, everything was becoming healthy again.

ANTHOLOGY

"Aye, Leo, did you pick up anything else besides shrooms? You know, any hard shit? Acid, LSD, DMT? Don't hold out on Jess and me, man, just 'cause Michelle don't want none."

Wow. JJ was either psychic, or he heard our conversation outside the car.

"No, JJ, I didn't pick up anything else. Strictly shrooms. Keep it safe and 'euphoric' for us all."

His eyes darted back toward the road, and he tuned out for the rest of the ride. Michelle held a stare for about five minutes but decided it wasn't worth the time and then looked back to the road. JJ crossed his arms as if he was pouting and sat in silence. Jess, heh, Jess was tripping so hard on the hash that she was passed out till we got there.

Time couldn't have passed slower, and thankfully, we had arrived. Leo turned the wheel, and the signage read H-ven Oak Campgro-nds. So that indicated as to how often people came up here. It really was our little escape from the world. Last year, the *u* was missing, and a year later, without repair, another one fell. I was just excited to finally arrive at our spot. You see, the first time we came up here, it was random. It was the five of us, and we had searched this whole campground for the perfect spot. Well, after basically scouring three-fourths of the campus, we finally found our ideal place. The spot had a prebuilt firepit of stone, and the view was to die for. As we rolled up, the sun was cleanly in the morning sky, shining down. I was the first to get out of the car. I needed to feel free. Like I was finally back in control again. As I stretched my arms like wings, I embraced the glowing light and knew today was going to be a great day. Hopefully. As everyone slowly got out, we began unpacking. Everyone had assigned duties each year, and this year was just the same. Leo and I set up the massive group tent. The girls would set up the grill, coolers, mats, and seats. Then JJ would finish by unpacking all the firewood and stacking it next to the pit.

The discussion quickly struck, and I reminisced on our first trips, the conversations that forged this bond we had, real talk too. Leo and I knew the conversation was for later for the sake of the group. So he and I chatted as we usually did and avoided the tiger waiting to pounce for answers. The girls were the first ones done, and they made jokes as we kept on working. Remember, I was residually stoned, so placing the hooks into the ground for the tent was one hell of a task.

"Damn it, not again."

"You missed the spot again, Justin?"

"Yeah. I might as well hand it off to one of the ladies. What do you think of that, girls?"

"Ha, in your dreams, stoner boy. Leo, go help him."

"I don't mind helping out. Justin looks like he could use a hand."

Damn, Jess.

"No, it's fine. I got it, Jess."

"No, you clearly don't. You're not used to the stuff JJ and I smoke. It's okay J., I got it."

She called me J. I'd never heard her say that before.

Anyways, I went to take my seat next to Michelle. Leo and Jess finished setting up the tent. Then I went to look for JJ, but I couldn't see him. The firewood was all stacked, but I couldn't see him.

"Yo, JJ, where are you?"

"I'm over here. Behind the van. Sorry, I was taking a piss."

Whew. Thank God. I was worried. I thought Michelle was too. I thought she knew something was up between Leo and me. It took us an hour, but we finally finished. We had most of the afternoon to go do something, but we decided just to rest so we could watch the stars and have the first trip tonight. We all tucked into different places. I found a perfect tree to pull my hat down and get some shut-eye. Leo did the same. Michelle and Jess slept in the tent, and JJ slept by the already glowing fire. The snow was cold, but we all had the gear to match it. All right, pleasant dreams. Good dreams. Think good things…

I awoke to black, but I was not awake. I was dreaming. Space. I was in the stars. It was beautiful. The expanse. You're probably noting something extraordinary now. You're perhaps questioning how I'm talking with you at this moment. Well, let me answer those questions right now. After all, in this dream, I am omniscient; therefore, I extend beyond this page into your psyche. So listen and read.

In this ocean of stars, there is a box. It contains a piece of something that should have never existed or created. It is merely a piece of the whole, and its properties provide it with...universe-disrupting power. He is the man who looks in our sleepless moments. He is the man who scavenges in an ocean of beautiful nothingness. Yet he manages to creep and molest through it without a care. Please help me. I know his name, but I can't recall it right now. I'm dreaming, and I need your help. He has left me here. I don't know when I'll wake up.

I'm trapped—trapped in an ocean of stars. I'm sorry. I never gave you those answers. Well, you're probably wondering why most of the time since this tale began, I have been sleeping during most of the events occurring, with simple explanations as to how the time has passed. Here is the secret, this could all be a dream, and we could possibly not even be camping on the mountain right now, but let me tell you—

"Hello, Justin. It seems you're trying to bring attention to some knowledge that only a select few should know. I'm going to send you back now. There's no need to be scared. Don't cry. Everything is going just swell. Now wake up gently, Justin. Wake up gently."

He's in my head. Oh god, get him out. Get him out!

The crackle of the fire woke me up as I saw the sun off in the distance beginning to set for the day. Time flew by. Couldn't say that I dreamed. I would've hoped I did. After smoking the stuff that JJ brought, I hoped for a pretrip awakening of some sort. I felt refreshed, better. I didn't know what had gotten into the wiggles, but I liked it. I walked toward the fire, and I was the last to wake it looked like. Leo was playing his guitar, serenading Michelle. Jess and JJ were still smoking, but they were listening to the sounds of the winds and creatures about. There I was strolling to the party, late as always.

"So we all going to watch the sunset on the cliff or what?"

"Hey! I was beginning to wonder when you were going to wake up. I know you've had trouble sleeping for the last couple of days."

Trouble sleeping? All I've been doing is sleeping.

"Uh, yeah. So the sun is starting to go down. Let's hurry. It's the tradition. It's always the first night tradition."

"We'll be right there, J."

There she goes again with the J.

JJ got up and sprinted toward me. I didn't know whether to brace for impact or a bear hug. Thankfully, the gentle stoner graced me with a usual hug and said, "Yo, man. We've been missing out talking with you all day. Come on, let's go watch the sunset."

Michelle jogged right past us.

"I'll beat all of you to it!"

I looked at JJ. "Race you?"

"Oh, you're on."

"Jess! Count us down."

Jess ran up next to us as we entered our sprint positions. Leo ran past us, so we skipped the countdown and hauled ass after him.

"Hey! Wait up, guys. Damn boys. Always leaving us girls in the dust."

Yes, Jess. Leaving you in the dust is what we are doing.

As we all reached the cliff, the winner didn't brag, but it didn't matter who won. We were all together for four years—four years of the fantasy friendship story. We moved to the edge of the cliff as we looked down across the valley. The sun had set for the day. We remained silent as we watched that last light beginning to descend, and it left us with a blissful feeling and painted sky. I looked around, and everyone looked at one another.

Leo spoke, "I love you guys no matter what. Honestly, I don't know who else I could call friends like you guys."

"Back at you, Leo. Even with all the bullshit, squabbles, and sometimes withholding the truth and being a minor douchebag, we're family till the end."

"Wow, that was quite heavily charged, Justin. Are you implying something about Leo?"

"No, Michelle. I'm not."

"Well, it sounds like you are..."

The silence returned, and JJ broke that quick, uneasy moment with a sudden burst of laughter. He was oblivious to the situation really at hand.

"Leo, let's go talk."

"Yeah...I was afraid you'd say that."

The three stayed as the final light descended fully, and Leo and I got up to go talk in a more private spot. The walk was pretty much silent for the first two minutes, so I decided to be the grown-up and talked first.

"Here good?"

"Yeah."

"All right, Leo, just tell me. All of it. Nothing but the truth. I deserve to know, brother."

"Okay...I've been lying to you all, Justin. I...I've been having some troubles lately, man. You remember when I said that I found out about Mr. Jacket through my brother buying shit from him? Sorry, I found out about him. Man, I've been exploring these drugs, and they've been...well, they've been expanding my mind and shit. Mr. Jacket has been there to help me out for the first few trips, and he's shown me things, Justin—things you couldn't possibly imagine."

His answer struck me, like it always did in these situations. I was shocked, but not surprised. Mostly hurt. I wondered why he hadn't told anyone about this. I wondered about this addiction problem. I mean, I knew his brother was a complete waste, but Leo?

"Leo, man. Why haven't you come to us about this? If you're having trouble with drugs and addictions, Michelle, myself, JJ, or Jess will help you out."

"No, you don't get it, Justin. After the things I've seen, they're just too beautiful not to experience again. It's not an addiction. I'm not an addict like my brother. Michelle wouldn't understand, so she doesn't need to know. I thought you'd understand because you've always got my back and I have yours. JJ and Jess? They're the real addicts."

"You're a fucking hypocrite. First, you think that Michelle wouldn't understand. Why? Because she recognizes it as an addiction when you see it as a hobby. And my case? Hell, man. You've been lying to me for how long about this? Bringing me to Jacket's place. Him taking advantage of me. Losing time like that. What the hell happened, man? I lay on the floor unconscious while you got high with your new stoner guide? Fuck you, man. You're turning into a waste, man. If you can't see that, then I don't know what to tell you. Oh, and you can forget about the shrooms and other hallucinogens. I'm going clean for the rest of the trip."

So there it was. The whole, hurtful, and burdening truth. Fuck. My best friend lying for months. His addiction to some harmful drugs was even worse than I thought. He was practically on another planet now. I was heading back to the campsite when I saw Michell approaching me from the corner of my eye. Leo wasn't in tow; he was still probably shocked about our talk and was sulking back in the wood.

"What's going on, Michelle?"

"Nothing much, Justin. Leo's just been an ass as of late."

"Tell me about it."

"Look, I normally don't do this, but I feel like I need to talk to someone about this. Leo's been so distant that I don't think I can rely on him that much for a response and guidance, and I was kind of hoping you would listen."

I really considered this for a moment because I didn't want to go behind Leo's back and listen to his girlfriend's problems. Then again, she was one of my best friends, and I wanted to be there for her.

"Look, I'm sorry I asked. I didn't want to make you—"

"No, Michelle, you aren't making me uncomfortable. I'm here. Listen, I'm here. Come on, let's talk on the way back to the campsite."

"Thank you, Justin, really."

"No problem, Michelle."

I wrapped my arm around her, giving her a hug. Sometimes that was all a girl needed. After what Leo had just pulled, I gave Michelle a little extra strength in that hug to make up for his lack of attention. We walked back, and she poured it all out. Michelle told me he'd been doing too many drugs and exploring dangerous things. He'd been hanging out with suspicious people. She was just worried about him. So I told her the truth. I told her everything that Leo had just poured out to me. She was not surprised to hear it. Her imagined concerns were all proven correct to everyone's misfortune. She turned to hug me, and the crying began.

"I...I...I thought I could help him, Justin. I really, really did. It's just been so hard lately. He's been so distant. I've just been so alone."

"Shh. Shh. It's okay. Leo will come around soon. I know he'll get some sense knocked into him. After all, with a girl like you, who wouldn't? You know how lucky Leo is? I bet he doesn't even see your devotion to him. It is so selfless and loving. I wish I had something like that."

"Do you really mean that?"

"Every word."

"Why does it feel like I've just woken up from an overdue nightmare and you were the prince to awaken me from it?"

"We can't."

"Who says?"

"Michelle..."

She pressed on me further, and I didn't even bother to look around for Leo. He betrayed both our loyalties. He deserved this. So I pulled her closer, and we kissed. My god, she was amazing. I'd had that fleeting thought occasionally *about Michelle*, but nothing ever like this. Wow, she was... Leo was an ass. As we finished that momentous expression, she and I looked at each other, and not a word was spoken. She wrapped her hand in mine, and we made our way back to the campsite.

It had been an hour since sundown, and Michelle and I detached our hands from each other as we approached. JJ and Jess were sitting there waiting for our return, surprisingly without any devices that inflict "euphoria."

"Where have you guys been? Come on, it's time for stories and food. We're starving here."

"I know. I know. We were just talking with Leo. I'm sure he'll be back soon."

I looked to Michelle. She grinned and then looked to JJ and Jess.

"No need to worry. We can get started without him."

"Suits us!"

Michelle and I went to the coolers and said we'd prep the food in the back of the car so we could snag the forbidden kiss away from prying eyes. JJ and Jess were assigned to making our cheap liquor cocktails from whatever we could find in our parents' cabinets. We were going about our duties, and still no sign of Leo, but I was not too worried. He was a brooder. Michelle kept pulling me in and out, slapping my butt, kissing me. She was a flirty one. I couldn't help myself around her. I sincerely didn't feel bad at all for Leo. He fucked up.

As we all regrouped at the campfire, there was still no sign of Leo.

Jess sparked the question, "Still no sign of him?"

"None."

"Do you think one of us should call his phone?"

"Yeah, I'll give it a ring," said JJ.

Michelle was holding my hand while my other hand was holding the food. Suddenly, I noticed through the darkness a figure approaching from across the campsite.

"Leo! Leo, is that you?"

No response, but I saw whatever it was approaching closer.

JJ and Jess began to shout at it, so I knew I was not crazy for not seeing anything. Still silent, but as the character moved into the light of the fire, we confirmed it was Leo. He looked pissed. He must be needing another dose. Withdrawals and all. Michelle decided to butt in now.

"Hey, asshole! Will you actually give a shit about someone other than yourself for once?"

His head remained down as he moved past us like a phantom. The fours of us thought he was dramatic. Leo's always been a dramatist. We went to huddle around the fire, now without worrying about where Leo was. We now suspect he was sulking on the trunk of the car. Michelle's tickling my hand now, whispering in my ear about naughty things. I played along, but really, I was enjoying the hell out of it. Jess and JJ struck a conversation, and we still went on without Leo.

Thirty minutes passed by, and now Michelle was sitting on my lap. Jess and JJ were taking another smoke break. That was when I saw Leo hop off the back of the truck bed. Michelle didn't bother to hop off my lap. I was sure it would cause a fight, but everyone seemed prepared to not deal with Leo's bullshit. He continued to approach silently, and I couldn't quite make out his expression from the flames. As he came up to us from across the flaming pit, I could now see his face. He was smiling, and the voice that came out of him did not belong to Leo.

"Justin and Michelle, you dirty, filthy little sex mongrels. What would Leo do if he found out about you two? Do you think he would slit your throats? No. I think he would peel the layers of your skin off, then he would dress them in mannequins, making them dance. No, too artistic. It needs to be more...what's the word? Ah, *primal*. How about a good old scalping and satanic sacrifice? Well, I know Lucifer wouldn't be happy to that, but who cares? This is for me anyway."

Michelle pressed onto me, expressing nothing but fear, and I could practically smell the adrenaline pouring out from her. Me? My best friend seemed to be possessed. I really didn't know what was going on, and all the booze and weed was making it hard to stay oriented.

So I asked the most straightforward question, "What have you done with Leo?"

As the fake Leo stayed across the way, the fire seemed to be pressed down by his presence, and a menacing shadow cast over Leo's face.

"I've done nothing with Leo, Justin. He's right here. In fact, he's ready to talk to you two. Oh my, I don't want to spoil the plans, so here we go!"

Leo's body fell back and dropped to the floor. I looked at Michelle, and I was not sure whether to run away or go check on our friend. My loyal instinct, hell, that was a funny one. I should say out of goodwill I felt compelled to check on our lost friend.

"Michelle, go get Jess and JJ. I'll handle Leo."

"Are you sure?"

"Yes."

She kissed me and told me to be careful. I grabbed a large poker stick we had been using, and I moved cautiously over to the fallen body of my once best friend. Now I don't know what he is. As I peered slowly around, I saw the fallen body. Leo still looked unconscious. I was going to try talking to him before I got any closer.

"Leo, you have to snap out of it, man. I don't know whether you were trying to scare us or if that wasn't you. Please I need my best—"

Like a mummy rising out of a coffin, he quickly jumped to his feet, and his eyes… Oh god, he had Mr. Jacket's same eyes—those starry, soulless things.

"Oh, I'm awake, Justin. Like I told you before, I've been expanding my mind! I've been at nothing but my best for the past few months, and Mr. Jacket has helped me realize the potential I have. After all, that's why we're all here. So I can finally experience the final truth."

"Leo, I don't know what the hell you're talking about. You can't scare me. And what the hell is the final truth?"

He approached closer, and I heard running footsteps in the background. It must be the others.

"It's quite a simple answer, really, Justin. It's nothing. It's absence. It's death."

I felt hands grab around my arm, and I turned to see the trio motioning for me to start running away. Michelle must have let them know. I felt paralyzed. I felt her pulling, but I couldn't move. Then it all began to tune out slowly—the nighttime noises, the screaming, the crackle of the fire. And I was a witness to the horror about to unfold. His gaze, it was like Medusa's, and I watched as he forced me to turn to see the others behind me. He touched me and put me in the place that he wanted me and then proceeded to do the same with Michelle.

"You see, there's this grand scheme, this great plan. But it's not the one you're thinking of. No, it's a lot more ancient than that. Life is entropy. And our reward is death. Welcome it! Now, Justin, see and watch. Explore the boundaries. After all, this will be the trip of a lifetime, my friend."

As he positioned a frozen Michelle, he moved her hands to point at herself as she was holding a gun to her head. Then he moved toward JJ. He positioned to have a knife pressed against his navel, pulling in an upward motion. Then finally, in sheer horror, I saw him pick up a helpless Jess. He picked her up and walked over the fire and threw her in. The silence was deafening at this point, and no screams from her skin charring and melting reached my ear. All I saw between the flames spitting and her frozen body was her tears singing close to her eyes. That was when I thought she realized she was dead. This would be the last thing she would see. I was helpless to the horror, and I was screaming. I was crying and shouting, but nothing was coming out.

Leo then moved to JJ, where he placed a knife in his hand. Slowly, Leo used JJ's arm to pull the knife upward. Blood squirted first, skin broke, then muscle tore, and his organs soon began to spill out. I couldn't even imagine the pain he was experiencing watching his insides fall to the pavement as he was frozen like a statue. So much like Jess, I saw it in his eyes as his life left his body. He was gone. A soulless muscle without substance. Leo looked at Michelle and me, and I knew he wanted this to be a moment of torment for the two of us.

"My two best friends. Of course, I had to save you for last. You two, after all, are the cheaters who've been hiding the truth from me. What? Did you not think that I was sneaking in the forest as I watched you have that silent moment of embrace behind my back? Tsk. Tsk. Michelle, I loved you, but I knew we weren't going to last. Hell, I couldn't really care for much at this point anyway."

My speech still locked; I tried to move any muscle, but it was like a signal sending without receiving. Le continued to place his dirty hands over Michelle.

"Have you always dreamed about this, Justin? The licking, biting, tearing, pain, pleasure, seduction, blood, sweat, fluid, embrace, love, passion with her? I know you have. You can't lie to me. I know all truths, and you are a dirty little liar. So here's what I'm going to do. I'm going to paralyze you, Justin, and you're going to have to choose…"

He picked up Michelle's frozen body and brought her over toward the cliff, and I was still frozen in place. Leo gave himself the time to make it slow and torturous, just watching. I was putting my entire will into writhing from his hold, but it was no use. He finally set her at the edge of the cliff and began his walk back. Within earshot, he continued his speech.

"As I was saying, I'm going to give you a choice. Like most decisions in life, it's one or the other, and this case is no different. So! Here. Is. How. This. Is. Going. To. Go. ALL THE WAY DOWN!"

He moved to pick me up, and with brutish strength, he threw me over his shoulder. He continued to just say insane bullshit.

"Justin, either you get to choose to save Michelle from being thrown off this cliff, or if you prefer, I'll release myself from this new expanse that has kept me! Tough decision, lover boy. Here, I'll put you down, and once I'm in position, I'll unfreeze you. I promise."

He set me down a generous ten feet away from Michelle. I was looking right at her and the tears of raging water dripping down her face. She was terrified, and all I wanted to do was save her. Leo was gone; I had to get that through my head. There was no redemption for him now. I must pick Michelle.

"So what's it going to be, J.? Jayboy? Justin? Lover? Cheater? Liar?"

He snapped his fingers, and I was free. Without even a second to consider, I knew my decision.

"I choose Michelle! I choose her."

"Aww, Justin. Did you really pick my girlfriend over your best friend? Tsk. Tsk. Tsk. I guess that decides it then. It looks like I'm the one going off the cliff. Or, to make this even more senseless, how about she and I both go, leaving you? I think that's a much more wonderful idea."

"No! We had a deal!"

"Justin, deals are meant to be broken, and the truth will always set you free. These are the only truths. Poor boy. You'll see."

I began to run toward Michelle, fearing Leo's threat, and I saw him in my periphery, lunging just the same. It felt like a millennium away, how far I was, but I needed to save her. I'd already lost all my friends; I just needed to save her. She was all I had left. If I was too...

I was too late. I saw his body push into hers, and as I reached into the space between, I sent my entire body flying in the last attempt to save what felt like a trial for my soul, but...

I'm always too late.

As I peered over the edge of the cliff, I saw the two falling like stones. With my hearing back, all I was hearing was the evil cackling of Leo knowing he'd won. The tears came flooding, and just as Michelle had said earlier, I felt more lost than ever. Maybe Leo was right. Maybe there was nothing after this and the only persistent truth in life was death. Hell, whoever saw this massacre would most likely frame me for all of it, being the last survivor and all. What was the point?

What. Is. The. Point?

I doubt I'd even feel a thing. So I got up, and I looked back at the bodies of my friends, knowing I'd fall into their hands once again. I saw Jess blackened, and I prayed for her soul to rest. JJ was finally resting, spreading himself onto the earth. And then there was me. I was going to join them.

I was nothing without them, so I took an invitation to plummet.

I was falling. I didn't know what was after, but I hoped I'd see her smile once again...

Fin

Chapter 4

Lyla Never Tells

They tried and trained us for these kinds of things—*interrogation*. We were taught never to give up anything. Absolutely anything we would say could and would be used against us, our fellow soldiers, and our country. I couldn't give a shit about the country I served. Hell, I was forced into the service anyways.

When they bagged me, I noticed the drive was a short one from the village my unit and I had been patrolling. That meant I couldn't be far from there. My captors must be holding me in a makeshift underground bunker somewhere in the buttfuck Middle East. They looked like ISIS, but they were organized, disciplined even. They still hated my guts, which hadn't stopped them from using crude and outdated torture techniques. And oh, do I fucking hate breathing sand and inhaling blood. So far, all they'd taken had been my fingernails. They told me they were just starting, but if this was how it was going to be the whole time, a special operation team should arrive by then and get me free.

I'd been trying to figure out what exactly their goal was here. I understood everything my captors were demanding, but I was in the Middle East, and my captors were speaking Portuguese. First deduction I could use to my advantage. Other deduction: their covered appearances, tattoos, and mannerisms I could reason they resembled Russian or Eastern European. Their accents were terrific, and that was the giveaway. That was the tell. Now I knew this had to be a setup. There was no way I was not here for a reason.

ANTHOLOGY

So let's backtrack to what I remember. My squad and I had been deployed on a simple reconnaissance mission, the typical shit-ass grunts were told to do, so it actually looked like we had a place here. Standard routine: two SUVs, fully equipped, six soldiers per van, and I was appointed squad leader, fuck me. Our CO was requisitioned to an alternate base yesterday. Just my luck. It was going to be a simple mission. It was supposed to be a simple mission, but need I say more? Our objectives were clear: sweep and check the small village forty klicks away. Insurgents had been reported in the vicinity but had recently vacated. Our intelligence got wind of the chatter a few hours before wheels up. They told us we would be in the clear.

We were sent to monitor the roadways and perform our regular checks for explosives planted in the road and perform additional recon for sniper coverage of the base. All in all, a general day out in the desert. Within fifteen minutes of wheels up, we were hit with two RPGs from nowhere. I knew it was an ambush. Intelligence had performed a digital sweep earlier and recorded small chatter, but nothing this big. The insurgents were recent. The timing seemed off, and that helped me now prove why I was here. Anyways, one rocket landed directly in front of transport 1, while the other took a direct hit to the driver's door. I was in the first transport when I began having our boys and gals deploy a defensive perimeter to take out whatever bastards had decided to attack us.

We were only a few klicks away from the base, so requesting backup cleared in my mind as the proper objective in this situation. I remember yelling a few orders to some of my men, for flank positions, but I saw them drop like stones when they were each taken out by sniper rounds to the skull. I was behind the cover of the passenger door when I started laying down some suppressing fire, still not having time to make the call. We needed to get ourselves together, but the noise was suppressing the communication severely. I began calling out to my squadmates to no avail. From the rounds being shot and sent forth to the artillery exploding, grenades igniting, and metal clanking, my ears were ringing with an intensity. I was screaming orders into nothingness. I was alone in this solace until I remember seeing a grenade.

It was a solid fifteen feet away, but I still needed to dodge for cover. Two choices: dodge to the open, most likely KIA'd by the incoming fire, or jump toward the pit below the grenade. Hoping to use blast wave and not concuss my brain too much, I would then launch into sandy dunes far below, away from incoming fire, thus giving me time to call in for backup. The latter was the best choice. So in a brazen move, I jumped as high up as I could and tucked into a ball. The grenade exploded. I felt not a shrapnel but a small wave pushing me higher, and there I was flying. I saw the incoming sand and began to roll. It was all a blur from there on out. I remember short but intense fiery pain, spurts of barking orders, and my dazed body dragged and thrown into a transport vehicle. There was not much else to the story besides those facts.

They'd decided to halt the beatings, lucky me. Now it gave me a chance to observe them. In one corner, a soldier was taking a piss. The other two were playing a game of cards. The wall behind me was less than a couple feet away from my tied hands. It was a small room in my observation. The fresh dust was dropping down fast like someone had shuffled it recently. A staler place would have less. These guys sure weren't insurgents. They were trained and most likely mercenaries, hence the voices not matching the picture. Between the amnesia and pain shooting through my entire body, I thought I was so worn down that the pain was actually not even subsiding. Instead, it was merely there, but invisible. I couldn't feel it anymore. What was wrong with me?

No one had come in since that torture began. I noticed the light fixated directly above the door when suddenly it was kicked open. No one stood on the opposite side of the empty doorway. It was like a ghost kicked it open, but that was not possible. It must have been the wind tunneling through the chamber. I saw the mercs settle down and return to their actions. Yet the door remained wide open. I had the means to a proper escape. I knew how to break these Boy Scout ties, but I couldn't predict what was beyond the door. These guys in here were no problem. It was the unpredictability that was going to get me killed. I'd just have to be patient and keep my mouth shut till then…

ANTHOLOGY

Be a good soldier.

As I stared at the wall, the dream of escaping was pushed to the depths of my mind. I began thinking about my boy back home. I didn't know if these would be my last moments, so I focused on the right things, pushed through the pain. My boy was back home; he was my little guy. His father and I split when I joined up. He cheated within two days of boot camp and left our baby boy with my mother. Ma didn't tell me till I graduated. Fuck Aaron for all he was, but at least I had been blessed with a beautiful baby boy. I had other obligations that needed tending, and my time with him had been brief. The Army had me deployed to this shithole, and my situation didn't exempt me from faraway deployment. So here I was, wondering if I'd ever see my son again. I knew he was either at school or he was with my mother right now. All I hoped for was his happiness and good health. As long as he was the farthest away from here. One of the soldiers playing cards decided to come over to check up on me. He raised his hand and let it down with force. The slap awakened me from the daydream of my son, but I wouldn't give him the pleasure of seeing my grief.

"What are you tearing up about there, you slut? You finally going to tell us what we want to know, bitch?"

He grabbed my face and squeezed it. He spat in my face, but that wouldn't get a reaction out of me. Fuck them and everything they did to me. They could have my body, *but nothing else.*

The setting changed rapidly with the unexpected entrance of someone I had yet to meet. The stranger was well-dressed and wore a mask. It appeared to resemble opaque ivory engraved with a simple pattern. Two upside-down triangles were marked below the eyes. His decor was sharp, tailored, and cocaine white—*Miami-like, not that LA death powder.* With each menacing step, the pace of my heart quickened. I was trying to keep myself calm, but I sensed the uneasiness in the entire room. Even the hired crew was shaking in their boots. I felt it in the floor, their heels tapping. My mind was aware and in control, but my body was telling me to run. What the hell was going on? He was so…silent.

He placed his briefcase on the table and reached with his free hand into his other pocket to pull out a cigarette box. He then turned to me.

"Hello, Sergeant Lyla."

I was gagged, so I was not able to reply, but I would tell this asshole that it was obvious to read a nametag.

"Care for a cigarette?"

I looked up at him, and I stared at his mask. There were no holes that I could see through, for it appeared to be pure ivory through and through. How could he see me, I wonder? He bent down closer to me as he brought his soulless expression to mine. He lifted the cigarette box and urged me to take one.

"Oh, I'm sorry. Will you gentlemen please undo all her restraints. We won't be needing them from here. Do try to keep her in the seat though."

As the men got up to untie me, I thought it best to not struggle. Let them undo the restraints, then see what they want to discuss. I believed they might simply just need to talk and then put a bullet to the brain. Make it painless and quick. Not some sadistic torture scene for the next few days, which I was sure this man could do. But I was not sensing that was his goal. Was it odd that I was genuinely curious about this character?

"Ah yes, Sergeant Lyla's mouth as well, please."

They finished untying my restraints, and I sat silently. The stranger watched me meticulously. He knew I was studying the scene. He knew it was a soldier's standard objective to survey any unfamiliar surroundings. He knew, and he didn't care. He was laid-back against a column, waiting patiently to see if I was going to talk.

"Lyla, please just tell us what we want to know, and this will all be over quickly."

"Stop calling me that."

"Does it bother you, Lyla?"

"No. Lyla's my civilian name."

"And what do you mean by that, Lyla?"

I jolted my head up in anger, but he was still unsurprised by any of my actions.

"What I mean by that is, I'm in the line of duty, so I'll go out as my name would be warranted in the line of duty."

"Ah, and why must that be Sergeant Naples? When I say Lyla, do you think of when your son calls you that? After all, you've only spent such little time with him. How could you know what your name sounds like when he speaks? You had to leave for duty all too fast after his birth. Your ex-husband raised him then gave him to your mother. He was still a baby boy when you graduated and returned home, but how long's it been, my dear? How long since you've heard the voice of your son? Eight…ten…fourteen. Ah, I think that's the lucky number. Fourteen months on deployment. Your boy, I would say, doesn't know how to address this woman any more than I would. I wonder how he perceives you. Is it Lyla or mother or mommy? I'm sorry, Lyla, but you know it's true. After all, the truth will always set you free."

He thought his words spooked me. He didn't know me. He couldn't *know* me. Yet I was a victim of his words. He knew all about me somehow…

"You're a bastard."

"A bastard I may be, but a liar I am not, Lyla. You, however, are. Now please, I was hired for a specific matter concerning events from a few nights ago. These events that have since brought to the attention of some, let's say, higher-ups would like to know exactly what you saw in concern with this event. Now, let's say, this situation that you should've never seen or even speculated about happened to be seen by you, which, in this case, makes it plain and simple. Simply tell me what you saw, and we will let you go. But there are two rules, my darling Lyla. Rule number 1: don't lie, because you'll know I'll know. Second rule: the truth will set you free."

In his relaxed poise, he waited for what he thought was my response. My brain told me to run for the door, but my heart told me to see my boy again. I was backed into a corner here, and I couldn't see a way out. So let us buy some time.

"Back during training, I got this little *saying* my fellow cadets started connecting with my name. They would see my perfect scores during interrogation training, under even the most difficult circumstances, and think, *Damn, that's one badass woman.* I was the woman who would never tell. 'Lyla never tells,' they would say. Guess what, here you have me, trying to break me like all the other men in my life, trying to have me tell you what you want to hear so that you'll get what you want. I know what I saw, and you know it too. Otherwise, I wouldn't be in this situation. What I saw was a direct violation of any and all human rights laws. So I'm not telling you jack because you already know those answers. Either get it over with or start negotiating."

He got up finally, something I didn't think he suspected. I just needed to rattle his cage a bit.

"Clever one, Lyla. You just got out of telling the truth by admitting you know the truth. Clever, clever girl. Well, that saves time on the first means of torture. Now onto the fun part."

He clapped his hands and moved toward the suitcase he had first set down on the table.

"Lyla, do tell me. Would you still care for that cigarette?"

If I was going to die here, might as well…

"Please."

"Excellent!"

He pulled out the same box and the same cigarette, handed it off to one of his boys, and shushed him away to me. The help even had the decency to light the disgusting, beautiful thing for me. What followed next…

"Do you know what this is, Lyla?"

I…I couldn't move. His action froze me. In the palm of his hand, he held a beating heart—a bloody, beating, throbbing heart.

"Lyla, darling, I need you to look at this here, please. I will ask again. Do you know what this is?"

"A…a heart."

"Yes. And who does it belong to?"

My throat clenched as fear gripped inside me. This couldn't be real. It had to be some trick. The heart was too fresh. It couldn't belong to anyone I know. I-it just…

"Lyla! I need an answer! Don't make me count down."

"I don't know! I don't know!"

"I told you before, Lyla, only the truth. I know you just lied, so I'm giving you a rare chance to tell the truth again. You have already lied twice. Another and you can't even begin to imagine what I will do to you."

"No! I'm telling the truth. I don't know…"

"Stupid, darling. You do know, but the stupid little voice in your head is still telling you not to tell. And why? 'Lyla never tells.' Is that why? Silly, foolish girl. That's strike 3."

He threw the heart at my feet, as my tears rolled onto it, and it finally stopped beating. The thumping halted, and suddenly, the sounds in the room fell silent. I looked up, and there he was, soulless.

"Lyla, that is your mother's heart. You know it, and I know it. Your boy is next. Children, unfortunately, are not off-limits. Now, Lyla, you have three strikes. Normally, I'd take your worthless life, but unfortunately, I need you. Sincerely, I do."

He turned to his hired help as I was fixated on the heart that was dead beneath me. I knew he wasn't lying. People like him didn't need to. They found more pleasure in telling the truth. The truth is more of a bitch than a lie sometimes. All a lie will ever do is get you into trouble.

"Gentlemen, your services will be enough for the time being. Take three of the four vehicles outside. Oh, and make sure to leave the one with the boy in it. I'm sure Ms. Lyla would like that."

As soon as I heard the word spill from his mouth, a furious rage burned inside. I leaped toward the towering stranger in a suicidal effort, but it was no use. I fell into perilous clutches. My breath escaped me as he slowly squeezed my throat shut. My desperate attempt failed, and now his hands were wrapped around my fragile stem, waiting for a flinch to snap. Unexpectedly, he let me go. My near-unconscious body dropped to the dirt below. I struggled to regain my breath as I saw the help follow his commands and leave the room. Now it was just the wall and me.

"W-will yo-u at le-as-t tel-l me wh-o you are?"

He took a step forward because he knew I was too weak to do anything, and he leaned down into my ear.

"Jacket, Mr. Jacket."

The escape mattered to me no more, for all I cared about was the safety of my boy. I'd do whatever I needed to secure that happening.

"Mr. Jacket"—I coughed—"please, I'll give you anything you want. Whatever you need me to say, to do, to report, whatever it may be, I will do it. Just…just please do not hurt my boy."

He placed his finger below my chin, and his mask stared right at me.

"Do you know what the truth is, Lyla? You see, I'm very old, and the truth has never been more apparent with passing age. There are plenty of truths. I've been witness to many. The most honest truths are the ones you tell yourself late at night, lying in bed with your lover, watching over your child sleeping at night. Those little events, they are the small truths that help make this beautiful lie we live in all the less painful. So, Lyla, the truth is this. You will die here, but not exactly here. I will leave you, the boy, and the vehicle. I will never see you again. This may all be made possible as long as you agree to one thing."

I looked up to the soulless man, and like the devil offering me eternal life, I took it sinfully.

"What is it that you bid me do?"

"It's effortless actually. Just look into my eyes, and tell me what you see. The eyes are the truest way to the soul. So please describe them to me in all their detail."

Whatever it takes, I thought. I nodded, agreeing to Jacket's bidding. He turned away from me as I saw his hands moving to remove the mask from his face. Once the cover lowered, he turned to look at me and asked his question.

"Lyla, what do you see?"

I looked into his starry gaze as an ocean of horrors flooded my mind. Imagine the horror of killing your own child because you were scared the world was going to kill it. Imagine the fear of burning yourself alive for thinking about setting fire to your neighbor's house. Imagine slitting your own throat because your husband told you how worthless you were in the kitchen. Imagine all the primality and terror of black-and-white truth. These and worse. His eyes burned into my synapses, and the pain was immense, but then I passed through it. I was sinking further into an ocean. The horror flashed, and now I was paralyzed in a sea of stars, floating in an absence.

A voice from beyond reached into this absence, and the discord vibrated through my skull.

"Is it not beautiful? The futility and fragileness of life?"

For a second, I thought he was right. I believed the lie. Or was it the truth? I was drowning. Help me…

I was sitting under a tree. The sun was shining with the perfect warmth. The sky was a vibrant blue. I held a book in my hand, and I put it down for just a second. I heard birds singing, and I saw the dance that my little boy was performing. He was giggling, laughing, and smiling without a care in the world, and I was at peace. I looked at him, and he, me. He ran to me, and as he got closer and closer, I could hear him calling, "Mommy! Mommy!"

I slowly began to wake, and Ethan's voice kept ringing in my ear.

"Mommy! Mommy!"

The screams, the pain already inflicted, the fact that the world was on my chest and I couldn't breathe made it hard to understand what was actually going on. The daze was humiliatingly sabotaging any form of clear intellectual thought from conjuring in my head. Then in the periphery, I saw little legs running to me. I was scared. I felt a push, but there was not much too it. I looked, and there he was, my beautiful little boy. Ethan. As he continued to try and budge me, I used all I had to hug him, and finally, I reached him. He tried to wrap himself around me, but he was still so small.

"It's okay. It's okay. Mommy has you."

I did. I finally had my boy.

Careless, though, I thought. I was too wrapped up in my emotions to even check my surroundings. Where was Jacket? We needed to get out of this prison. I picked up Ethan, and I told him it would be all right. I looked down at the floor and noticed the heart that had been thrown at my feet. I remember what Jacket said. *I'm sorry, Mom. If that really is your heart, I'm sorry for leaving it here. I have other priorities now.* I told Ethan to hold on to me as I picked him up. I finally walked from my tiny box into a hallway. I saw the light at the end of the tunnel, and we ran toward it. There were no doors along the hall, so I didn't worry about checking my corners. When we finally reached the end of the hallway, the light was bursting through, and I heard nothing that could indicate danger. Jacket must have taken the last vehicle, I thought. Where else could he have gone?

We came out of the tunnel, and the light blinded my eyes; I almost dropped Ethan from the bursting rays. I carefully set him down as my vision came back. There was a car not fifteen feet from where we stood, and before I could even speak, Ethan ran toward it. That must have been what they brought him in. *What the hell am I thinking? Run after him. Don't let my boy run in this desert alone.* I reached him, picked him up, and got closer to the car. I checked inside the vehicle, and I observed no sign of anyone. I tried to unlock the door, and the handle budged willingly.

We had our means of escape, but where was Mr. Jacket? How did he escape? I looked behind me, and I didn't see any signs of that soulless man. Ethan then tapped my shoulder, and I couldn't help but be startled by his words.

"Mommy, where is the man?"

What did he do to my boy?

"What man, sweetie?"

"The tall one. White. White. White!"

I turned around again, fearing he was going to be there waiting. Thankfully, no man crept behind me in this killing field. Then again, what was I saying? I never wanted to see that monster again. *Consider this a miracle. Turn on the car, and get you and your boy home.* Common sense would start coming back to me once the superstition subsided. Then I actually stopped to consider that I had no clue where we even were. I must find a phone or something. I quickly finished strapping Ethan up into the back seat of the car and boosted his seat with Kevlar vests stacked in the back.

I moved around the edge of the car as a thought pierced my head. They used my son to get to me. Children were the kryptonite for parents' fears and anxieties. *Damn them.* I continued to move around the back of the car and headed to the driver's seat when I turned the corner and saw him. Silently, he stood, and not a millimeter of movement from him as he stared at the sun. Exactly as he was when I first laid eyes on him—his mask on and the terrors that cascaded around him. I could desert him, but what if that was what I was supposed to do? What if he was going to call in my escape, and then it was the end…?

Wait! He asked me a question as to what I saw when I looked in his eyes, and I never gave him an answer. He said Ethan and I could be free if I gave him the truth as to what I saw when I looked into his eyes. The scars that I would never forget. Could I possibly retell that horror and survive again? *Get it together, Lyla! This is for you and Ethan. Go! See the soulless man and end this. I promise I'll be back, Ethan.*

"I love you. Mommy will be right back," I said as I decided on my action. I marched across the dunes, and the tall man in white didn't bother to turn around. He already knew I was coming. He was expecting…

"I expect you're here to give me your answer, Lyla?"

How could he…

"Yes…I saw nothing. I-it's an absence."

"Yes. It was nothing, wasn't it? Can you describe it to me? I haven't heard a description of it in quite some time."

"Is that why you wear the mask?"

He then turned to face me.

"What mask?"

I looked at him, and still that stone-cold ivory face was unforgiving.

"You-you're wear…no, you're not even wearing a mask because it's you, isn't it? You're—"

"If your comparison's name begins with either *S* or *L*, then you're entirely wrong, Lyla. Everyone always gets it wrong. You're no different. What you see is a mask, and it's not a mask to me. It's my face. Well, at least the face I wear with you. Ethan saw something entirely different. Why do you think he ran from you back to my vehicle?"

No. That must be a lie. He…

"Stop talking in your head, Lyla. I can hear all your thoughts, darling. Secondly, you've been denying the truth and dodging the answers the entire time we've talked. Please pay attention and accept it."

"Why me?"

"I can. It's entertaining to play games. You're all a game."

"There's not a word to describe you, is there?"

"If there was one worth knowing, I would tell you, Lyla. It's the least I could do. Thank you for Ethan, by the way. I've been waiting for a boy like him for a long, long time."

Rage swelled inside my chest, and I wanted to harm his black soul for even thinking about my boy. Instinctually, the last primal act to lunge in anguish was extinguished quickly by Jacket's disappearing act. It began falling, tumbling, swirling, all of it. Suddenly, I was falling down these dunes, and the sand was stabbing me at every impact. I'd done everything I could, and it wasn't enough. My boy was no longer mine, taken from me by a phantom.

I would die alone, alone and forgotten in sands older than time. Was this my punishment? Was this the time that I'd spent in my final hours? Wasteful...

I felt a quick snap in my back as the tumbling continued, and half my body switched off. The acrobatics didn't cease as I thought the gravity loosened its grip on me. The stop came slowly, and I realized I couldn't move. My legs didn't work anymore. Another broken, wasteful thing. Alone at the bottom of a godforsaken pit.

Goodbye, Ethan. I love you.

I closed my eyes, and the light slowly began to fade. It had been four days and six hours since they'd left, and the vultures had torn me to pieces. I was just alive enough to tell you that the truth was simple.

Mr. Jacket would come for you. *When you see him, look the other way.*

Fin

Chapter 5

Is Life Worth Living Without You?

This week had been hell already, and it was only Tuesday. Dad had been running around with his ex-con acquaintances again. The worst thing about that? Gambling. He began owing guys more debt still. He didn't do jack but drink and watch TV. Hell, he hadn't even thought to earn back any of the money owed. If he did earn any from the poker games at Randy's, then it all poured itself back into the booze.

The bastard couldn't even screw his head on when he woke up from his stupors. I didn't even do a damn thing when he pulled out the belt twice this week. Apparently, he just lost his nerve, his damned nerve. His damned drinking was the problem. He let the guilt rot him from the inside out, and it had been this way for however long I could remember. The rage that burrowed deep inside him always surfaced at some point, and he took it out on me. Most would think it was because Mom left long ago, but she escaped at the perfect time. She wasn't trapped here like I was.

My only escape was outside the damn place. No matter how long I spent away, I didn't feel homesick. One month ago, my girl Daisy and I took a road trip up to Canada. We wanted to get some fresh mountain air and smoke a little grass she had grown. When we got back, Dad barely noticed that I was gone. Goes to show you how much he cares.

That was just the beginning of the week. To make my plate even fuller, Daisy gave me some bad news last night while she and I were grabbing a bite. The trip to Canada? Well, there was a little more than just fresh air and some hash. The lovemaking was beautiful, but we were far from safe. It had been almost a month since we got back, and she had been telling me she hadn't been feeling good the past week. I thought it was just her standard period, but I guess it turned out to be another answer. She'd taken a pregnancy test before school that morning, and she told me the result was positive. The news shocked me, but my heart or my head spun. My mind focused instead of falling apart. My girl had summoned the courage to tell me the news immediately after she found out; it was harder not to fall deeper in love with her.

The news, despite the shit week, brought up my spirits. The girl I loved was going to be the mother of my future child. I reached to give her a hug, but she just stood there, motionless. My own joy overwhelmed me. I completely forgot we had to return to class. The bell struck, and she held my hand and looked at me with her cute expression. A little tear formed, but I wiped it away. I kissed her forehead and told her everything was going to be all right.

After a busy day of classes, the slow roll of thoughts continuing to build in my head finally decided to tumble down. Before I knew it, the dread hit like a hammer to a skull. I practically fell down the staircase on the way to sixth period when it all hit me. Daisy came first to my mind. My poor girl, she was pregnant at seventeen and would have to carry the burden of having a baby. Hell, our parents would kill us before term even came. That was if they ever came around. The thoughts rattled off in my head. *What if she wants to keep it? How can we raise this child? How can we support this child?*

The final bell of the day rang, and I rushed to my car to meet Daisy. Thankfully, I was her ride home for the rest of the week. Her parents were both out of town, and I felt a little relieved knowing she and I would have plenty of time to talk. As I pushed and shoved through what seemed like the entirety of the school's population rushing toward the parking lot, my perception of time slowed. Did I fear the imminent dread, or was I preparing to comfort when I also needed soothing? I finally burst through the bubble of people and made way to a clearer path. As I reached into my pocket to grab my keys, my pace picked up. I wanted to be first in the car, but I looked up, and I could see her. She was already at the passenger door. Her expression painted somber like Mona Lisa. I walked up slowly, trying to judge the scene.

"Hey."

"Hi."

I went to give her a hug, and she let me in. She hugged me tighter than at any time ever before. She turned to look up at me and spoke, "Everything's going to be all right, okay? We're going to get through this. Together."

Every urge in my body was telling me to run from this, but I pulled her closer and said, "No matter what. Together. You and me, baby."

How little we knew back then, how little we anticipated what would unfold in the next *ten minutes...*

The tension in the car was absent. She sat there, one hand in mine and the other holding her belly. She smiled and let the sunshine down on her through the windshield. The sound of the wind quietly rustled by, and I heard the humming of an angel next to me. We were almost to the town center when she gripped my hand real tight and looked to me with all seriousness.

"I need chocolate."

I cracked a smile.

"Do the cravings really begin this early?"

"Does a man get to tell a lady what she eats?" She giggled and gave me the mischievous wink. *Damn, I am in love with this girl.*

The grocery store was two turns away, so I made the quick detour to abide by my ravenous girl. As I pulled into the tiny parking spot, she gripped one more time with a slight flinch and asked if she could come in with me. I always ended up picking the wrong thing, and she knew it too. I tugged her arm a little to let her know. "Come on."

As I walked around the back of the car to unlock Daisy's door, I noticed a somewhat standout character directly across the street at the Green Patton. Early afternoon and this gentleman was drinking what looked like a Jack and ice. He was tall as could be, wearing shades darker than space, and was doused with oil and grease. He knew I was glancing at him, and he raised his glass to me. I simply nodded back. I reached to open my lady's door, and she was giddy with anticipation.

"Do you remember which one's my favorite?"

"Well, we're here for chocolate, aren't we?"

"No, silly. I'm talking about my favorite type of chocolate."

"Oh…isn't it—"

"Bzzzz! Wrong. Time's up."

"Hey! That's not fair."

She made it to the door, and I followed quickly. This girl had me wrapped around her finger, and she knew it with all her heart. I entered the store and saw her little feet shuffle toward the sugar aisle. I was in the same corridor seconds after chasing Daisy down. I peeped around the corner, and she was already diving her hands into the multitudes of chocolate. I couldn't help but smile when she turned to see me standing helpless against her expression.

"What are you waiting for? Come, help me."

Do as the lady asks, I thought to myself. I headed down the aisle when my ears suddenly went deaf. For less than a moment, a ringing pain burst my eardrums. I opened my eyes from the quick stabbing pain and saw Daisy experiencing the same agony. It sounded like a gunshot.

Daisy looked to me, and I recognized the fear swelling in her eyes. I ran toward my girl, and I tried forming a plan of action, but I'd never been in a situation like this. I moved my finger to her lips and asked Daisy to be quiet. I threw my jacket around her and told her to move slowly. *Just head toward down the exit of the store,* I thought. Two more gunshots echoed in our ears, and this time, they sounded closer.

At the end of the aisle, I peered around the corner and saw him in my periphery. The same stranger I saw outside was now wielding a gun. His expression emoted terror. His eyes were deep and hideous. He was yelling at random, shooting at random, and I placed Daisy directly behind me. He approached closer, and we had nowhere to go. We were stuck between the exit and a madman.

I made a call. I put my hand up, making myself known, and I pleaded.

"Please! Let us go. You don't want to do this."

Unfazed by my actions, he stepped closer. His voice crept into my ear, and it made me twitch. The cold, frozen language formed from his lips, "No, no, no. Thattttt just won't do. I like *her* more than you. I think I'll take her, and you can go. If you don't move, then I'll just drag you along with us. Maybe you'll have to be missing a few parts, but who cares? You look like quite the hefty fella anyways. Maybe we could shed a few pounds."

Daisy was gripping my back, and I was pretty sure she broke the skin. The terror rose, and I was caught in its grip. I acted out of pure survival. I lunged at him, and a shot rang in my ear. I dropped to the floor and felt a pool flowing. I heard Daisy beginning to scream as warm, hot red blood began to flow from the wound. Right in my gut, I could feel the hole. I was going into shock. I could not black out. The crazed man slowly approached my helpless body and bent down, placing the gun in my mouth. The iron was cold, and I could smell the oil and powder.

"I'm not going to kill you because that would make it too easy. No, I'm going to take your girl right here, and she's going to be mine. *If you survive,* then come find us. She may not be the same, but I think you'll like the…well, the adjustments I'm going to be making. Ha!"

Daisy's screaming barely rang in my ears as I could see her knees quaking. The terror had frozen her, and I looked at her helplessly. She wanted to come to my side, but the hesitation was halting her. The gunman removed the gun from my mouth and looked up to Daisy.

"Hey there, darlin'. Say, why don't you take a ride with me? We can go someplace quiet. Maybe even open up the fun box. Oh, who knows! I may just kill you after I'm done taking care of that beautiful body of yours."

The gunman then looked down to me and pointed the barrel directly at my head.

"Any last words, partner?"

He pulled the trigger without hesitation, and the ring from the shot burst an eardrum. In the deafening echo of the bullet, I turned to see the hole in the floor. It was less than an inch from my head. The pain rang throughout my skull, hindering any movement. I was overwhelmed by the blood gushing forth as everything slowed. I saw the bastard grip his hand around my baby girl's arm, pulling her toward the exit. Somehow, I found it in myself to get my first knee up. I wouldn't let him take her. She was all I had in this world.

Between the fades of black, I pushed through the pain. The shelves helped keep my body up as I pushed myself along them. I followed the blood trail dripping from the man's outfit. I swore if that bastard hurt Daisy in anyway…

Focus, goddammit. Get your girl back. Just keep moving. I saw the red neon sign labeled Exit, and I pushed my entire body through it. Thankfully, the railing caught my almost-helpless body from laying itself on the street below. As I got my grips, I turned my head and saw them. The gunman was putting her in his car. He must've parked it in the alley before he entered through the front. I tried to yell, but my voice was choking in the middle of my throat. *Keep pushing, goddammit. Get to the car.* I saw him throw my Daisy in the back seat as he turned and saw me hobbling over to him.

"My, oh my, do we have a resilient one here. What are you going to do, Romeo? You can barely stand. You can't release the pressure from the wound. You can barely stand from your eardrum bursting. Ha, please, oh please, keep hobbling. It's noble but utterly pathetic."

He waved his gun at me as he slowly moved toward the driver's door. Sirens were echoing in the background. He timed his escape perfectly, and here I was, always late, always behind the curve. I continued my wayward journey to the fading green car. I could see him slowly starting to pull away. I couldn't hear, I couldn't stand, and I was not even sure if the car was moving at all. Then I saw it and knew it was not just a figment of my confused mind. The end of the alley approached for him, and I was left in the dust. I fell, and the ground shoot pain throughout the rest of my failing form. As I saw the car begin to turn out of the alley, I saw Daisy looking through the back window. Her mouth was taped, and she appeared to be screaming.

All I wanted to say was "I'm sorry that I am not enough," but words couldn't even begin to form.

I caught the last glimpse of my darling girl when the unexpected again entered into the fray. The sound was indescribable, but the action was total. An 18-wheeler going down the street had just hit the gunman's car. It T-boned the bastard's car directly into the building, crumpling what used to be a vehicle. As the ground shook and the building quaked from the impact, I saw the car hanging by pounds of loose sheet metal. My mind screamed because my Daisy was in the back of the gunman's car. Sirens were still a distant echo, but I couldn't wait for their arrival. I felt arms beginning to pick me up from underneath my pits, but I didn't bother to turn around and look at my aide. I was still fixated on the incident unfolding before me. Between the flashes of consciousness, I could barely make out what the man pulling me from the event was yelling.

"It's...to...get away! Get—"

I saw Daisy's body open the door, but it was crushed against the wall of the building. I saw her mouth scream for help, still covered by tape, as rushing bodies ran toward her. Then the flames became visible. A trail of gasoline leaking from the massive hauler was pouring into the driver's side door, and the spark was catching up. The men running toward my girl suddenly halted. They knew there was no time, but my mind couldn't stop screaming. There I was being pulled away, and my Daisy was about to be sent into oblivion. I saw my darling banging against the glass when it finally broke, but it was too late. The flames raged slowly, forming a ring around the car. In those last moments, I made out some words falling from her lips, "I love..."

Then it was over. Glass windows shattered down the alley. The heat from the tanker exploding was a giant ball of rage and fury. I felt my eyes slowly melt into my skull, even when my brain was telling me to close them. I couldn't bear to look away as everything I had ever hoped was gone in a flash of pointlessness.

The sirens were here now as medics were pulling me into the back of the ambulance. The building began to crumble onto the wreckage below, and I knew there was no hope for anyone in the fallout. The man who pulled me away was an officer arriving on the scene. He was trying to talk to me, but I wouldn't look away from the terror raging ahead.

They strapped me into the ambulance and began to close the doors as my response to my love's last words couldn't even pierce the exit of my quivering throat. The tears came, and the pain swelled.

It's gone. Everything, all of it is gone.

My world had been a singularity of ruin since I'd woken up from my nightmare. The doctors told me that I was induced into a coma to reduce the suspected damage that might have been caused to my brain from the blood and oxygen loss. The doctors and nurses tried comforting me, asking the routine questions. Still, between the fades of in-and-out consciousness, I couldn't bother to respond. Words rang and bounced, but what was the point?

"Do you need anything?"

"Does this make it more comfortable?"

"Would you like our in-house therapist to come see you?"

And all the rest. I was too tired to respond. The other thoughts brewing inside were ones that should just be kept silent, buried. They didn't need to come out.

A day after I woke up from the long sleep, a few police officers visited my room.

"Hello, this is Detective Mohan, and I'm Detective Darcy. We've come to ask you a few questions about the incident that unfortunately unfolded on March 21. Your name is Robert Jameson, correct?"

I didn't want to speak. I could barely find the will in me to, but I must. It was best to know what had happened since I'd been "dead" for so long.

"Yes, that's my name."

"Well, Mr. Jameson…"

"Robby…call me Robby."

"Okay, Robby. Post-incident, you were obviously unavailable for questioning due to your injuries. And therein lies the problem. We had nothing to go on to flash any light on this atrocity. The three persons involved were all incapacitated or deceased…"

The word *deceased* drilled itself into my brain. Daisy...

"We had to shelve it until you regained consciousness for the whole story. The only information we could gather was a statement from the only attendant working at the store. He only saw you stumbling through the back to go after someone. We presume the gunman and his hostage. Our conclusions state the gunman shot off two rounds into the ceiling of the store with zero threats or demands. He then proceeded to walk up and down the aisles where I presume he found you?"

I caught only the end of the officer's discord, and I hesitated to respond. Was I really the only one who knew the story of Daisy and my demise?

"Yes, sir, that would be correct."

"Look, I know this may be hard for you, son, but I have a case to close. I need you to focus, all right? The quicker we get this over with, the quicker my partner and I will be leaving you."

Six months with an unsolved cold case. The paperwork must be horrendous. I couldn't even begin to imagine the pain this officer would go through with the simplest task.

"You want answers, well, here you go. It was a senseless act of violence that took the only light in my life away from me. The result gifted the earth's dirt with another homicidal psychopath whose sole mission was to destroy an innocent couple's lives with no purpose except bloodshed and chaos."

I turned to look at the window, but the shades were still drawn. *These bastards. To have the heart to say that to me. They can't imagine what I'm going through.*

"All right, kid. How about my partner and I reconvene when you're out of this morbid place? We'll buy you some joe, and we can talk about the minutia. Get some rest, kid. You've got a lot to get through."

Then it was silence again. The detective's footsteps barely made a sound on the way out. All I wanted to do was sleep and never wake up. I knew that was not going to happen though. Not in here. I returned to staring out the shaded window, imagining what lay behind, and I slowly drifted back into the warm clutches of the void.

The door opened to my room, and I was awoken to the doctor.

"Good evening, Robby. We have some good news. After bringing you back from the coma, it seems your brain's swelling has gone down excellently. Your blood has returned to normal saturation, and we removed all the possible chances of infection through administered antibiotics in your IV during your sleep. As it checks out, you'll be good to go by tomorrow morning. We'll keep you overnight for insurance's sake. Good night."

Before I could even summon a word, the door closed, and once again, I was left alone. I turned my head away from the entrance and returned to my curtains when I saw a figure sitting in my visitor's chair. He sat silently. His demeanor and stature were both stoic and silent. His white hat tipped down as if he was asleep. I couldn't seem to take my eyes off him. Where did he come from? How did I not hear him?

"Hello, Robert."

He halted my thoughts. Or at least that was what it felt like when he just spoke.

"W-who are you?"

"Let's save that for another time, maybe a little later. Robert, I have something I want to ask you."

I was becoming tired of the charades.

"No, I think I deserve to know your name, seemingly since you know mine. Who are you to come here? Do you even know why I'm here? The...the person I lost."

He began to stand up from his chair, and as his head tilted up, I saw the embroidered mask adorned on his face.

"Your questions will all be answered, Robert. Patience is a virtue after all. Now, my dear fellow, as I asked before, I have a question for you."

"Fine. What is it you'd like to ask, stranger?"

"If I could grant you anything you wanted that has been lost, what would it be?"

"You have to be joking with me."

He couldn't be serious.

"Deadly, in fact."

His expressionless gaze drilled more profound and deeper, and I didn't want to shake it. As I looked deeper, I sensed no deception. There was no lie, I could decipher. I couldn't even recognize any form of emotion from his expression. Then the thought surfaced to my mind, and I knew what answer he was expecting now.

"You know the answer already."

"I do, Robert. I just need you to speak the words yourself. Self-profession is the key to this here deal. A deal is nothing without a man's word. His word is his testimony to the truth and nothing but."

"A hearsay? You can't expect me to believe what you say. You offer me all I want to hear, for what? The exchange of my soul?"

"Do I look like an entity interested in your soul, Robert? Please I'm not a demon of any sort. I simply just want you to answer the question in words of your own. All I ask is, your answer beholds nothing but the whole and honest truth."

I dared not look away. The stranger's expression remained serious. I did not doubt what he said, but could he actually do it? Could he bring her back? I didn't want to even think about the way they must've buried her. She had to have been cremated. That…disaster…

"She won't be the same, will she?"

"No, no, no, Robert. You have it all wrong. She will come back even more perfect. A newly flowered Daisy, one could say."

He knew everything I could ever want or wish. Why was I not afraid of what he was offering? He would fundamentally change everything if he did fulfill it. Why was he offering me this?

"Why me, stranger?"

"Jacket. Please call me Mr. Jacket."

"O-okay. I need to know why. Why did you choose me? Why am I so special?"

He moved now to my bedside, and I saw his wrinkled white velvet glove place itself on the railings of my bed. I should be afraid, but I was not.

"It's simple, Robert. You've been chosen. No, not by a higher entity but by me. I can give you everything you could ever want, but only once. There's the catch. One time only. One wish, and you have to believe in it, Robert. If you don't, then consequences form."

"Consequences?"

"Yes."

"C-could you ela—"

"Yes. You must put your belief into this wish, Robert. If you waver at all, then it will crumble all around you. Now do you want her back? Do you offer absolutely anything to have her back?"

He knew that I would do anything to get her back, but I couldn't seem to believe what he was saying. If he could really bring my baby girl to me, then she needed to perfect. I wanted to think he could. I needed her back. My life would be nothing without her. I thought it would be better this time around, a second chance, another life to begin again.

"She'll be exactly the same, right?"

"Pieces of the whole are not the whole. She will be whole, yes."

"O-our baby?"

"No, Robert. I told you, just one wish. You never really wanted the baby, did you? You always wanted her above everything else. Admit it, Robert. She's all you could ever want and need. That child was nothing but another string that needed plucking."

As he continued to just stand over me and spoke so resolutely, my mind began forming around the words propelled into them. Everything he said, I…I believed it.

"Daisy…I want her back."

"Perfect. When you leave here tomorrow, go to the gardens in central. You will see a trail of orchids and sunflowers. Your Daisy will be at the end of the trail as beautiful as she was the day you lost her."

"T-that's it?"

"Yes, what more would there be?"

"You're telling me that once I leave this place tomorrow, that I will walk to the gardens in central and at the end of the path I will see my Daisy?"

"Yes. Daisy won't even remember anything from that terrible day. Consider that a gift from me."

Tears began to run down my face, and happiness swelled forth. I reached to shake this man's hand, but he swiftly removed it from my bedside. I saw him beginning to walk toward the shades.

"Once I open these shades, Robert, you will wake up tomorrow. You'll sleep through the rest of this silent night and dream of Daisy. She will blossom by tomorrow, and then it will be Robert and Daisy forever. Now rest..."

My eyes slowly began to shut, and I listened to his trance. After all the terror that I bore witness to since I lost her, I'd finally be able to see my girl again.

With the shades to my room finally open, the morning sun peeked through. After a dreary and dreaded week of lost hope drowning in a black abyss, I felt a tiny spark ignite in my heart. The ordeal yesterday was not cringing in my belly; in fact, Mr. Jacket was giving me everything I could ever need again. Despite the one minor loss of our child-to-be, Daisy and I would be together again. We could start over.

The morning quickly went by, and I was finally signing the discharge papers. My dad hadn't even bothered to visit the entire time I was in the hospital. He didn't even think to pick me up. I wondered if he knew where I'd been?

I got into the elevator to exit the hospital as uneasiness faded away and the spark continued to grow. The clock ticked inside because each passing second brought me closer to my girl. As Jacket said, "The gardens in central."

As I exited the rotating doors swinging people inside and out, I passed through the blue skies and sun pouring on my face. After the gloom of lost time, I was ready to begin again. I saw a taxi, and I waved it over. He flashed his high beams and started driving over to me.

"Could you take me to Central Gardens?"

"Sure, it should only be a twenty-minute drive. Hop in."

"Thanks."

I'm coming, Daisy. Only twenty more minutes, baby. I hope you're not bothered too much by not remembering much. I'm sure you'll have questions about lost time, but Jacket said that shouldn't come up. In fact, I don't think I'll even bring it up. We can start fresh, brand spanking new.

The car ride was mostly silent, and the city sounds rang strange in my ears. I hadn't heard them for quite some time. With one blown eardrum and the other with its perpetual buzzing, I was sure my hearing was nothing from what it used to be. As the taxi turned right toward the Gardens, I eagerly shook in my seat. *It's like no time has passed since I've lost you.* The cab stopped and pulled to the curb. We had arrived.

"That will be $17.80, please."

"Here, take a twenty and keep the change. Have a good one."

"Thanks, I hope she's excited to see you."

I looked at him with a surprised expression.

"H-how did you know?"

"Mate, you've been jumping in your seat the entire time, with a smile bigger than the bridge. It has to be a girl."

"Yeah. She's the girl. She's the one. What can I say?"

"Good luck."

"Heh. Thanks."

I closed the door to the cab, and I headed into the Gardens. Now I needed to find the trail of orchids and sunflowers, just as Jacket told me. At the end was where I'd find my Daisy. That was what he said. As I walked deeper into the Gardens, I saw the trail marked Orchids, and I beamed directly toward it. I followed the path, like purple and yellow painted the scene. Dandies of petals flew effortlessly in the wind as the fragrances reformed memories of how she used to smell. I passed through the opening to see a park bench and a beautiful open lake when I saw her. She was in the same white dress she was on the day of the… *No, don't go there.* She looked stunning as she simply watched the fountain in the middle of the lake. I should approach slowly, only in case I startled her. I began to move forward as I picked up the tunes silently escaping her mouth. She was humming her favorite song, "Daisy, Daisy, give me your answer true. I'm half crazy over the love of you." The lyrics barely escaped her lips, but I remembered it was her favorite. The time lost dissipated along with the flowing winds, and I finally approached her and spoke, "Hi."

She turned around to look at me, and that same old smile formed across that face of hers. Her cheeks burst into red cherries, and her eyes opened more vast than an ocean's horizon line.

"I've been waiting for you, silly. You told me twelve. It's half past."

"I-I'm sorry, Daisy girl... It-it's just..."

My hand placed itself against my face, and I didn't know whether to cry or to hug my girl. Could it possibly be true? Was Daisy back?

"Hey now, don't get all mushy on me, lover boy. You know that's my job."

As the lone tear began to form in the corner of my eye, I finally let it fall.

"It's been so long, Daisy... I'd never thought I would see you again."

"What are you talking about, silly? I saw you yesterday. I visited you after the accident. Remember, I brought you your favorite chocolate doughnut from Singh's."

To my memory, that never happened. I rolled with it. I'd tell Daisy later.

"Yes! Sorry, the drugs must still have my mind all fuzzy. I've just missed you so much."

She got up from the park bench, and as I watched that pure white dress flow from the low rumblings of the wind, I was attracted to her even more so than ever before.

"Well, are you going to come here? Or do I have to come and get you?"

I let more tears rush down, and I finally embraced my girl. Six months. Six months I'd been "dead," absent from the world around me. *Six months without you, and now I finally have you back without a scratch. Daisy, I promise to you that I'll never let you go again.*

"You're very silent today, Robby. Is there something on your mind?"

"Just you."

Her smile grew even more prominent, and she wrestled her arm in between mine. We began walking. Nothing needed to be said, for we just walked in each other's arms as the glorious sunshine doused down upon us. We walked and walked, and the silence was beautiful. Finally, I was at rest.

After about an hour's stroll through Central, we exited. Daisy said she had begun feeling grumbles in her tummy. I thought it best for us to head to our favorite diner on Dander Street. The diner's name was Tonya's, and it was the classic American dream—24-7, fresh pies, black coffee aromas throughout, dirty aprons, and of course, the lovely old waitress, Éclair. I hope she was still there. As we strolled through the streets, I just couldn't resist being happy. After those days of loneliness and finally the offer from Jacket…

Zero consequences. I could not believe it. There must be a catch, I thought, but I couldn't bother to think about them. My subconscious could continue to scream all it wanted. I was too busy focusing on my girl to listen.

Daisy rushed into Tonya's as that familiar *ding ding* rang in our ears. I heard ol' Éclair yelling at us seconds after.

"Wow! Where have you two hooligans been?" She cracked a smile drawn with the utmost sarcasm.

Daisy replied in kind, "Well, Éclair, it's simple. My boy and I have been hopping down to the diner on Eastle Street. We'd hoped you noticed our disappearance and called the police or something. I guess you aren't very good at checking in on your regulars."

The snarky banter between the two ended in a gigantic hug, and I was left waiting for mine.

"Robert! My dear boy, come on, don't be left out of this."

I joined the ever-growing bear hug unfolding and was embraced with warm feelings. After the brief hellos and catchups, we headed to our regular booth. Daisy loved the seats in the corner because they overlooked all four corners of the street. Daisy loved to see the abundance of cars and people all zooming by. The buzz of the city was her favorite noise. She'd always been fascinated by the little things in this world. I wished I could say the same. Daisy peered out the window into the world that she lost and had since found again when I felt the existential dread beginning to unravel itself. Jacket's offer surfaced, and my gut sank. I hadn't even considered anything besides those and Daisy and I reconnecting. Then I thought about my father again. Did he know I was missing?

"Hey, Daisy?"

"What's up, sweet guy?"

ANTHOLOGY

"I...I think I need to check on my dad. I have just this...well, awful feeling."

"Did this just start, Robby?"

"No sooner as we sat down did it begin."

"Well, we better get going then. I'll apologize to Éclair and tell her we will see her soon. I'll meet you outside."

I almost forgot how organized and focused Daisy could be in intense situations. She was always the one to calm me down. Thank God I had her back. As I saw her get up to go see Éclair, I flashed a wave goodbye and headed outside. Daisy was not too far behind as I already saw her move her hands to her mouth to call a taxi. I helped her put on her coat, and a cab rolled up promptly. We entered and gave the driver directions.

"To 347 Shedwick Street, Manhattan."

"Gotcha."

The ride was silent. The rumbling of tires on the road and the mild radio buzzing was the ambiance. Daisy looked between the city and me as she squeezed my hand intermittently. I could tell she was worried, but she always put on such a strong face. The ride passed by quickly, and as we pulled up to my neighborhood, I saw why my stomach felt like there was an anchor sinking in it. Two police squad cars, one ambulance, and one fire truck all parked directly outside my house. I looked to Daisy, and she saw the same as me. We paid the driver in silence as we exited. I paced my way toward my home. I approached the caution tape being propped around the car as I notified one of the police officers that this was my home.

"This is your house, son?"

"Yes, sir. Has something happened?"

"I'm afraid so, son. You were living with your father, correct?"

"Yes."

"Did you know he'd been using some illegal substances within your household?"

"No, sir."

"I'm sorry, kid. Your daddy seemed to have overdosed last night between 11 p.m. to 1:00 a.m., at least that's what the coroner boys are saying. Do you mind if I ask where you were last night?"

His words hit me like a tidal wave. It all came flooding in now. Daisy remained blank, for she had no recollection about any events from the last six months. For all I knew, she thought it was six months ago. Hell, I was in the hospital yesterday. How would I explain that one?

"Son?"

"W-whuh? Oh, sorry. I was entered into the hospital last night."

The officer and Daisy both looked at me, utterly confused.

"You were in the hospital last night and didn't tell me?"

"Why were you in the hospital, kid?"

The bombardment of questions overwhelmed me, and to make matters worse, the thought of my father passing began to swell in my throat.

"I-I'm sorry. I'll explain in a few. May...may I see my father?"

"I don't think you want to see him, kid."

"Why not? He's my dad."

"Kid...I-I don't know how to explain this, but...well, before he died from the overdose, he left a very morose message. It wasn't a handwritten note either."

"I need to see him."

"All right, all right. I know you'll regret it."

I looked to Daisy, and she squeezed my hand tighter. Her eyes told me she wanted to be there with me. She knew my dad, and I had never been on the best of terms with him, but she knew this was different. I lowered my head underneath the cautioned yellow, and Daisy remained tied as we waded through the maze of officers, trucks, patrols, cars, medics, and CSI. I reached my front door, and it was already open. I walked into the living room, and on my left, I saw what the officer outside meant by letter.

"JaCKeT MaDE Me" was painted across the wall in black and red liquid. I saw my father's body directly beneath the bloody fingerprint trail as the body bag already covered his lifeless body. I didn't want to take a step closer because the man I once knew was gone. Taken from this world. *Taken because of me.*

The regret that had been anchoring in my stomach all day had now reached its climax. The deal I made last night... There was no doubt that this was tied to this. The urge to throw up swelled upward, and I aimed for the bucket conveniently placed in the hallway. As I hurled, all the pain from the day I lost Daisy reemerged in my mind. The shattering pain, the withering loss, and now I realized the consequences of my deal.

Daisy tried comforting me, but I needed fresh air, and I quickly darted outside. Once I made it to the porch, I saw him—the tall white ghost of a man towering on the other side of the street. He looked directly at me and remained motionless. He froze my soul with a single glance—a glance I would never forget. A car rushed by, and in the afterimage, the sidewalk was empty.

When Jacket asked me to abide by the truth and nothing but, I did. I told the truth when I said I would do anything to have my Daisy back. The truth that never came forward? What would I give to have her again? The deal was two-sided; I was just too blinded to think about the other. A life for a life…an end for a beginning.

So tell me. Was I the luckiest guy in the world? Or was I one of the many who had fallen to the disease of humanity?

Fin

Chapter 6

Jungle Fever

I didn't know what I was doing.

No one could have seen what was coming. We thought it was going to be a typical anthropological study. Claire and I had done them a thousand times before ever since our days in university. Those days were behind me now. Claire was gone. I left her back there.

They were savages, bent to the will of a man's voice. He spoke, and they listened. The Uganomie tribe had welcomed us in. We were among them, observing for almost a week before all this. There were signs that we shouldn't have stayed. We…I didn't listen to them. It was my fault. It was my fault that she was gone. I was a coward. As soon as trouble showed, I ran. I hadn't looked back until now.

I stopped by a large tree erecting into the broad daylight and remembered the tortures of the jungle. The humidity was drowning. I was practically shedding pounds by the second. My heart was racing; it felt like it was beating a hundred miles an hour. I needed to calm down. There was no point in dying of a heart attack. *Okay, think.* How did this all start? I quickly padded across my body; I remember placing my journal in one of my pockets earlier. I felt around the back, and there it was, perfectly tucked away. I opened it, and my sweat had burrowed into the bindings. The pages were wet, but it was still readable. *Okay, start at the beginning.*

"We arrived on Monday and set up camp twenty-five yards from the tribe's central hut. It was early afternoon when we arrived. The sun was blazing that day. The farther we walked from the road where the driver dropped us off, the hotter it was. Claire and I pushed on though. This was our chance to nail our thesis on an almost-mythological tribe of nomads. I'll remember to thank Professor Knowles for setting this whole thing up when—"

The rest of the ink was too smudged from the running. It washed the impermanent ink away. Hold on, it picked up further down. The fluid hadn't spread as deep as I thought. Wednesday, okay, that was where I could begin.

"The amount of research that has been wrong about this place, my god. Everything Claire and I read in the prepping for this trip haven't been proven right. The most exciting aspect we have observed is the arrival of their 'god.' From what we can translate, or try to, his name is Jacket. His body alone strikes your eyes like a piece of paper. It's bleached white. His entire body is simply otherworldly. His mask—I definitely need to get my hands on it—is one of the most beautiful and intricate pieces of ebony I have ever observed. Since yesterday, he hasn't moved from the cliffside. He's been sitting in a meditative state, *uncovered*, in direct sunlight. I tried to get closer to observe him carefully, but the tribe's chief halted me in my tracks. He waved his spear repeatedly in my face until I began to step back. Claire had made the observation that maybe this man is a god when she was smoking earlier in the day. I scoffed because God doesn't exist. More on this later…"

My god, I could barely remember writing any of this! What did they do to me? I thought about what happened two days ago, but nothing came to the front. What was wrong with me? It must've have been the drugs. It had to be. That was the only reasonable answer to this insane trip. There had to be some hallucinogenic substances in the root. Claire had been smoking it since…well, I think since we arrived and introduced ourselves. The words were coming, but the pictures in my brain weren't forming.

A rustling in the green woke me from introspection. I looked around and noticed not a thing out of place. Everything was dense here. The greenery alone was the size of pythons. Wading through this mess, trying to escape, was one hell of a task. I checked again, just one more time, in case there was something I missed. I was second-guessing myself now. If I did that any longer, I'd succumb to this madness. I wouldn't let this jungle infect me like Claire!

I took another look around real quick, and I headed forward. I needed to keep moving. I'd have hit some form of town or highway at some point. I just needed to keep pushing forward. I stepped through the abundance of weeds and roots that had covered the floor of the jungle. By how much there was, it looked like a buildup from centuries of untamed growth. This place felt ancient, powerful even. It was almost trancing, only by running through it.

I didn't want to believe everything they told us. The stories they spoke of… Ancient men ordained to serve their god. Cursed with an eternal mission to serve the truth. Knights of cruel and rigid standards. It was terrifying when the elder spoke of this man, this Jacket. He was a knight by belief or through passed down history; he was considered as the judge of the land. Jacket was the silent man. He rarely spoke according to the elder Claire spoke to. I remember she was talking with the elder when I was observing him. God, it must have been hours I stood there. What was wrong with me? The dehydration alone could have killed me.

The thought burst in my brain, *How can I remember all this about one man but not my own memories of our stay?* The question rocked me to my core. I feared that I'd been infected by the same indoctrination performed earlier. I…I wasn't supposed to wake up. It was too soon, I thought. I remember them trying to hold me down as I shook free of their grasp. The sacrificial altar that was next to mine was empty. Where had Claire gone? I woke up, and she wasn't there.

So I ran like a coward, and I fought through the crazed man, never a thought to look back. Yet all this occurred while the bleached man observed from the cliffside. When I replayed that scene again in my head, he appeared closer each time. He couldn't be doing this. This wasn't possible. I was caught completely off guard when I heard a rustle of the wind. I felt a pinch in my neck like a mosquito had just bitten me. I reached, and there was no insect. I pulled a small object from my skin and look at it. It looked like…

I awakened at the same altar I had escaped before. The fire raged in front of me. I felt hazy. They must have shot me with some form of poison. Everything was coming back, but slowly. I was trying to force my eyes open as one of the tribesmen came to me.

"Hello, John."

No, it can't be.

"Claire, where the hell have you been? Why are you...what is wrong with your skin?"

"Nothing's wrong with her skin, John. In fact, she's perfect in my eyes."

His voice pulsed through me. His words switched the *on* button to my foggy brain. The man named Jacket came into view as the shadows from the fire danced around his chalked body. He came closer, and I was terrified at what he might do.

"Now, John, I need you to do something for me."

"P-please let me go. I-I-I'll do anything you ask. Just please let me go."

"Do not cower in fear, John. You have nothing to be afraid of. I'm simply here to enlighten you. You see, I knew you and Claire were coming here. I knew you wanted to observe my tribe. I bet you didn't expect all of this. It's my masterpiece."

"Then let me show it to the world! Let me go. I'm more useful alive than dead."

"Ha! Men like you, John, they sure do make me chuckle sometimes. Isn't that right, Claire?"

"I think that's right, my love."

Love? What has he done to her? She's mine!

"John, you're getting this all wrong. I love my children. Claire is a recent member of this community, yes, but she saw the truth quicker than you. You have thought about moving closer to observe me, have you not?"

How did he know all these things?

"I know many things, and you're not paying attention, Jonathan! Now I'm going to ask only once, for I do not repeat myself, ever. Do you still love Claire for who she is despite her rebirth?"

I barely had time to think as the truth burst forth.

"No. In fact, her skin reminds me of death. I have no des... Stop. This. No, Claire that—"

She punched me in the face. My vision flashed momentarily when a second one came faster than the last. A final blow landed below my chin as my eyes rolled backward. Next thing I knew, blood came spilling from my mouth. I coughed and more flowed. What had he done to her?

"It's not about what I did to her. It's about what she did for you."

"Stop! Stop this madness, please! You can't know I'm thinking. Y-you just can't!"

"Oh, I most certainly can, John. Claire, please bring me the ceremonial blade. You see, I'm going to give you a second chance. One of those is very rare in my little rule book, so don't squander your chances."

I saw Claire grab the blade from the same elder I remembered her speaking to. She bowed to pay her respects and turned back to face me. I then set my eyes to Jacket, who stared expressionlessly into me. If I were a God-fearing man, I'd say he was looking into my soul.

"You are a fool, John, to think a man can't stare into another man's soul. The eyes, John, those are the windows into one's soul. It's the reason I don't have any. Truth is the only sight I need. So here's your second chance, John. Have you loved Claire since the first time you've met her?"

"How could I? You can't love someone until you know them. I met Claire on a blind date. I had no idea I was going to fall in love with her down the road..."

"Ah, so you are capable of telling the truth. Good. With that settled, I guess it's time for Claire to reveal her truth. Claire, my darling?"

"You're right, John. You can't love someone till you know them, but guess what? You can't love someone if you never knew what love is. That's my little secret, John. That's the one that Jacket finally helped me set free. I can't love, John. I know the word, but the emotion never came. I was hiding from who I was. I was stuck playing games with men like you—men I used to play with to hone my predatory nature. I've never cared for you. In fact, the only real positive of this whole debacle? This unshackling you brought me to. It's by fate. It seems that I'm freed here."

I was speechless to her crazed words. This wasn't the girl I knew. T-this couldn't be.

"Claire, please. Lis—"

I felt the blade inserted into my stomach. She looked at me dead in the eyes as she slowly began to pull it upward. The pain was so excruciating that I could barely form a word. Instead, I was forced to watch as she finished her ritual. She backed away as everything faded to black. She danced in the fire as shadows formed around her. Not long after, I felt the release. I knew my time had ended. Before my eyes closed forever, I saw her dancing with her savior…Jacket.

Fin

Chapter 7

Funeral for a *Lover*

"Bobby was the love of my life... We are here today to lay the man I loved to rest. There's... I'm sorry..."

There were just so many words I wanted to say, but none of them wanted to come out. The swelling of my throat immediately summoned tears to my eyes, and I saw Angela rush to be at my side. She knew how hard it had been since Bobby passed. *I wish I could say even a few words. I genuinely do, Bobby, but not right now. It's too soon. I don't have the strength. I'm sorry.*

I looked at Richard. He was the only other attending member of my husband's funeral. Four of us. That was all his soul had touched. It hurt. It hurt knowing he could have been so much more. The side of Bobby that I saw. The one he, unfortunately, always locked away when he left the house. Outside he was known by a different name, a name that was revered. That was why Bobby had no one here today. He was a fear mongrel of the business world. What was even scarier was, people never thought to act against him, because of the rumors surrounding my Bobby. Bobby truly loved only one thing in the entirety of his life. I hoped he did, at the very least. I'd like to think I changed him a little, but now I'd never know.

Angela rubbed my back, and Richard looked on. He was looking through me like I was a phantom. I knew he didn't want to be here. It was sad. I wished Bobby and Richard had worked everything out in the end. Since they were kids, the two were inseparable. Then

Angela and I came along, and it became the four of us. *Up until four months ago*. Bobby and Richard got into a fight one night when the two of them were out drinking. Some unpleasant mojo was thrown around; words were spoken. Some words, I would say, should never be spoken, from what Bobby told me. Actions were taken, and they left quick, stabbing scars. Angela never figured out what happened, and neither did I. The two barely said hello when they crossed paths after that. It was a shame. From then on, if anyone of us went out, it would now only be a trio rather than a quartet.

Then this happened. It was just so quick. No one could have predicted it happening. Angela and I were out at Chello's on Main having a girls' night when we got the call. The police were the ones calling. Bobby…died in our home. The emergency caller begged me not to visit the scene, but I needed to go see my Bobby. I told Angela immediately, and we both rushed to the car. I didn't think I even stopped for a red light on the way home. Red lights glared in my eyes as I drove past in an aura of silent speed. The anxiety building up inside had me seeing green instead. I sped the entire ride home. As we pulled up to our home, neon blue and red flashed off the house's white paint. It painted a scene no one ever hoped to see.

The ambulance personnel was already wheeling Bobby's body away, and I tried to burst through the crowd of people. Yelling, screaming, kicking, I tried everything I had to get past the restraints called men. Then as the ambulance drove off with Bobby's body, I collapsed. All that energy spent, for what? A bucket of tears and a swollen throat. Angela was just there and hugged me. I cried and cried. Neon blue and red just flashed on and on, and I was gutted by the knowledge that he was dead. I lay on the asphalt and watched as my tears sank onto the earth. Angela hugged me and told me that everything was going to be all right. But how could everything be okay? Was there any way to move on from this? Within minutes of the ambulance taking Bobby away, Richard pulled up to the scene. As soon as he got out of the car, he saw the two of us and ran over. He pulled us both together and even began to cry. Then the three of us sat as the rain started to fall on an already dreadful day.

It had been a week since that night, and the three of us hadn't even begun to recover. The shock still vibrated relentlessly through us all. After a week of tears and crushing regret, we have now arrived at the day where he might finally be put to rest. Here we were, burying the love of my life six feet under. I moved toward the black rectangular resting place, and I kissed the lid of his coffin one last time before they lowered it onto the cold ground. The tears from my face dripped onto the piano-black surface and glistened. *Heh, a little piece of me to be with you down there, Bobby.*

"Rest in peace, my love. You were my light in the dark tunnel, and now I hope you lay at rest knowing you'll see me in the end. I love you, Bobby."

I looked to the only official attending, and I nodded. He responded in kind and began lowering the coffin into the dug-out dirt. As Angela held me and Richard stood opposite, we looked in silence as the tomb was laid. This reality we lived in, the lives we touched, the hands we held—it was moments like these where those sweet things fly away, and all we were left with was the lonesome and cold touch of regret and pain.

After the funeral, Richard, Angela, and I all headed back to our home. I thought it best I was surrounded by the people that Bobby and I both loved with our entire hearts. At the house, I prepared food and drinks in quiet as the other two set up the table. Dinner was set for four out of habit by Angie. When I saw the fourth plate at the table, I couldn't help but tear up. Angela asked me if I wanted it to be removed, but I said, "No, he would've wanted it there." We sat and ate, mostly in silence. There wasn't much to say, so I struck up a conversation.

"Do you guys remember when we went to the carnival last year?"

Angie responded quickly, "Of course we do, sweetie. That was one of the most memorable days in years."

"Yeah, I remember that day," Richard replied.

That was the day Bobby proposed to me. It felt like we had been together for a lifetime already, but on that day, he finally sealed the knot that I had roped around him since the day we met. It was the happiest day of my life, maybe even better than the wedding. The conversation didn't stick, so the silence recommenced. I removed myself from the table and went to go clean up for the night. Tomorrow would be a new day, and I knew Bobby would've wanted me to look at it positively.

"Oh, Bobby...why'd you have to go so soon?"

In the kitchen, I placed my plate on the counter, and I just sat on the corner and cried.

Angela and Richard remained in the other room, and I heard the murmurs of a conversation. Still, I didn't pay close enough attention to listen to what was being spoken. They knew how to clean up the house, so I got up, and I decided to head to bed. Once I was upstairs, I undressed and aimed for the bed. I just needed to rest. This day, it had been too much.

The light burst into my room as the dawning sun rose. I turned to look at the clock, and it read 6:28 a.m. I cursed myself, "Dammit, I forgot to close the blinds last night."

As I pressed my hand against my face to cover the blinding light, I moved to close the blinds. It was too early. Bobby would've wanted me to rest. He'd known how much of a toll this would take on me. He was always the most understanding. As I untied the rope that held the shades in place, I quickly unfastened them so I could return to my slumber. As I finished untying the last drape, I turned around, and I caught a glimpse of a shadow rushing by the door. A piece of me wanted to go see where the shadow had come from; the other thought told me to return to bed. I defied the latter and moved toward my bedroom door. I quickly opened it up, but the hallway was empty. No sign of anyone there. It must have just been my imagination. I wondered if it was Angie or Rich; they could have stayed the night. I let the thought flee my mind, and I returned to the empty bed. It was time to rest.

Loud knocking awoke me once again, and this time, it was unrelenting in its fashion. I heard the murmured voices of someone trying to speak through the door, so I quickly moved to get out of bed. As I opened my bedroom door, the sounds became more transparent, and I moved to the staircase. As I turned the corner, I saw my front door was already wide open, and the sounds seemed to be coming from my living room. I rushed down the stairs without a single thought of the possible danger that might await below. Again, I turned the corner to see Angie and Rich on the couch, talking to two guests. I moved to close the door when Angie spoke at me, "Mori! I was hoping you'd heard the knocking. A few officers from the station wanted to stop by to ask you a few questions about Bobby. I hope you don't mind that I let them in."

I was not sure what to say. Why would the officers want a word so early?

"Yeah… Angie, did you make some coffee? I think I'm going to make some coffee."

Before I could turn and head toward the kitchen, the officer sitting in Bobby's old chair turned to look at me.

"Ms. Ash? Would you mind pouring my partner and me a couple of cups?"

He smiled, and it put me at ease. I looked to Angie one more time, and she was sitting with an embarrassed expression. I winked to let her know it was okay, and she smiled back at me.

"Sure. You are Officer…?"

"I'm Detective Branch, and this is Detective Craft."

"Pleased to meet you, ma'am. We'd hoped this visit would be on better circumstances, and we send our sentiments toward you and the family."

"Thank you."

I headed toward the kitchen to make the coffee when I heard Angie asking to be excused. I thought about how silly that was. Angie asking permission to go to the kitchen. She'd always been a rule follower. I thought that was why I'd always been her more fun opposite. Richard must like that order thing; he'd always seemed so…structured. As I entered the kitchen, I heard rushed footsteps approaching. Before I could turn around, Angie hugged me from behind.

"Hey, I'm sorry. It's the middle of the afternoon, and I would have totally wanted you to rest, but when I answered the door and saw the officers…I just didn't want to turn them away, you know?"

The fewer things changed…

"Angie, it's okay. They must be here for a reason. Thank you for letting them in."

She continued to squeeze, and I returned in kind. Angie had been my best friend since birth. Literally, we were born in the same hospital, two rooms adjacent to each other. It was as if we were destined to become friends; sisters, I dare say. She finished squeezing and set me down, at least pretended to. I could finally go prepare the coffee. Thank Jesus.

"You know it's terrible to keep our men waiting."

"Moira, please, they can wait as long as needed. For God's sake, you were just widowed."

Then it hit me. The officers were inquiring about Bobby's death. They must have decided on the ruling. Earlier this week, I attended a meeting at the police station asking about the possibility that Bobby was murdered. I couldn't think of anybody who would kill him. Still, I also told the detectives interviewing me, "My husband was a businessman, and he was…callous, monetarily speaking." Bobby never cheated anybody, but he also never took anyone along with him. He was a lone wolf, and he never needed to kill his prey, because they had respect for what he did, especially how he did it. A kingpin without the crime. This entire time, Angie had been speaking to me, and I hadn't even noticed.

"And why can't they see that you're hurting? It wasn't a murder. It couldn't be."

If Bobby did really love me, then I knew he would have never killed himself. He was a prideful man, and he always broke through the worst. There was just no way. Then again, I couldn't imagine why anyone would want to kill him as well.

"Angie, let's just finish with the coffee and get back to the room."

"Mori, are you all right? Seriously."

"Why? Do I not look all right?"

"No, hon. You don't."

Angie was honest. I loved her all the more for it. She could see past any barrier I put up for the crowds. She knew how deep down I didn't want to admit the truth.

"Yeah…you're right. Let's talk after this, okay? We have guests."

"Okay…thank you. I know I can be a lot sometimes…just, you know, thanks for opening up."

I bumped her shoulder as I headed back to the living room, and I winked. She was practically my sister; I could never stay mad or get mad at her for long. Once we reattended the meeting in the living room, we stumbled onto the detectives heavily questioning Richard.

"The night of the incident, Mr. Heath?"

"I was at home waiting for my wife to get home. As I'm sure Moira told you or your fellow officers, earlier this week, Moira and Angela were out on a girls' night."

"Yes. This is a confirmed fact by both women. That doesn't mean much though, especially when we have another source—a source trusted by the department."

Richard sharply noticed my entrance and Angie's following. His posture remained cooled; I could sense he was very annoyed by the detective's interrogation.

"What source would that be, Detective?"

"I'm afraid I cannot give you that information, sir."

"Just call me Richard."

"Sure, Richard."

The two detectives were heavily eyeballing Richard. Angie was quiet for the first time in ages, and I was so dull to the situation that I couldn't really care.

"Richard, I believe that Detective Branch and I would like to bring you back to the station for some more questioning, without your wife and the widow present. No offense, ladies."

Angie responded hastily, "N-none taken, Officers." I just nodded. It was not worth the energy. Richard looked at Angie and me, and he appeared neither innocent nor guilty. He had an emotionless expression. My judgment wasn't the best right now anyway. I was barely trusting my own words at this point. I was just so tired. Richard was not seeking approval; he saw it as a waste of time. I knew Richard could have never done it. Despite all of his and Bobby's differences, they were brothers. The farthest from Cain and Abel as possible. Angie would agree to the same.

Richard stood up and spoke, "All right. Let's just get this over with."

"Thank you, Richard. Sorry to ruin your Saturday, ladies. This shouldn't take more than a couple of hours. We'll even return him for you two gals."

"Thank you, Detective."

Angie looked on, and for the first time in a while, Angela Ash was speechless. Richard left silently. The detectives didn't place him in cuffs; that would undoubtedly help Richard's pride. Angie and I looked on as he now entered the detective's car. He didn't look at us; he looked at the passenger's back seat. As Angie and I looked on, an unsettling chill rushed up my spine. An ugly thought crept into my head. *Maybe Richard did do it.*

I returned to bed and let the ugly thoughts creep their way back into my subconscious. I couldn't bear facing the reason as to why or how Richard could be capable of such a terrible act. I returned to the bed that had become my only place of solace. I needed to sleep off the thoughts that I decreed forbidden. Angie needed Richard. She would fall apart without him, just like Bobby and me. Did I even feel guilty for pushing them to be together? Would I feel guilty for having my best friend's lover be imprisoned for the murder of her best friend's husband? The thought of hurting Angie or Richard was just not in me. After experiencing the same pain that I was going through, I couldn't double it for them. I couldn't decipher any of the thoughts going through my head, and the sleepless nights were driving me insane. I needed rest, but the world wouldn't let me. It just wanted to continue bombarding me relentlessly.

I quickly passed out from the mental exhaustion, and the endless internal questioning ceased for a few blissful hours of sleep. A few hours went by, albeit in a hazy half-asleep state when I was awakened to the sound of the front door closing. Murmurs of Angie's voice followed, and I assumed that Richard had just returned from the police station. I slowly began to move from the bed so I could hear what went down at the station. As I gathered my pajama bottoms I conveniently left thrown by the bedside and put on Bobby's old Zeppelin shirt, I looked at the reflection in the mirror. For a second, I saw someone standing behind me, a phantom, barely even the corner of a person's being. I swore I was hallucinating from sleep deprivation. I'd worry about my ghosts another time.

After throwing on my things, I headed downstairs to an already bustling situation. Angie seemed to already be drilling Richard. As I entered into the living room, Richard's eyes darted toward me like an arrow in an open field. I felt shot by his sight. Angie continued her ranting, and I stepped in to ease the situation.

"Hey, Rich, you just got back from the station. I bet you may be hungry. I think he may also need some time to relax. Don't you think so, Angela?"

Angie then darted her eyes toward me, but she knew I was right. There was no point to continue yelling. It just made matters worse. I was more worried about Richard at this point. He hadn't even spoken a word since entering back into the house. I matched his gaze to discover he never took his away from mine. The tension was building in the room, and now the situation was becoming unreadable.

"Don't you have anything to say, Richard? For Chrissake, there's—"

Before Angie could even finish her sentence, a sharp and muffled shot rang delicately in everyone's ears. I looked down at Richard's lap to see him wielding a gun. I looked at Angie, and there she was, standing in shock. The blood slowly began to appear through her white top, and she moved her hand to feel the pouring warm liquid. Without even a thought, I lunged to Angie's side to make sure she didn't fall. As she began tipping backward from the blood loss, I cradled her in my arms. Richard moved from Bobby's old chair. His gun was still aimed at the two of us.

"Moira, please move away from the whore."

"Richard, stop! Stop this nonsense. What the fuck are you doing? You just shot your fiancée! Put the gun down!"

"I'm afraid I'm not able to do that, Moira. You see, you and I need to have a conversation. See, I'm already under pressure from the cops, and you and Angie are only going to make it worse, so I'm going to need you to step away from Angie so I can finish this."

"Finish what? Do you even realize what you have done, y-you fucking bastard?"

"Angie, stop. Just stop. You know why all this is happening. You already know the answers to everything."

As I cradled Angie's body, the blood poured freely into my palms. Richard shot her in the gut, and soon I'd be drenched in the blood of my best friend. Richard's voice echoed, but I was deaf to the tone. My terrible, terrible theory about him was all coming to light. How could this even be possible?

"I know you're still piecing the puzzle together, Moira. So let me make it a bit easier for you. See, I made a deal, and that deal has almost come to fruition. I just needed to remove some players so that you and I would be alone."

As his words were processing in my head, the pieces came together. My mind toppled from the information unfolding. The shock was trying to make me freeze, but I wouldn't let it. I needed to save Angie. I needed to get out of here. I needed to distract Richard. Before I could even act on this half-assed plan, I felt Angie's hand reach into mine. She had let go of her wound, and I could see it in her eyes. She was passing. Richard placed the shot, and he knew where to put it.

"I-I-I'm"—she coughed—"sorry, M-Moira. J-just know I-I-I love…"

As life left her eyes, the tears came rushing forth, and once again, I was left alone—alone in my home with a madman. There was no need to plan an escape anymore. Richard was in full control, and he knew it. I closed my sister's eyes for the last time, and when I looked up to Richard, I saw his hand lifting. My vision went black, and the previous thought that escaped my mind before I passed out was, *I'm going to kill this man…*

The dried blood across my forehead had moved down between my eyes. I saw the crusty and hardened globs of red from the blunt trauma inflicted on me. Then I felt them, the zip ties that Rich must have found in my kitchen cabinet. The one's Bobby always used for quick repairs. My hands were separated through multiple restraints, as well as my feet. My vision came back slowly, and I could see the monster sitting directly across from me. His gun was planted on the table next to the chair that he sat on.

"I know you're awake, Moira. The twitch a body makes when it regains consciousness, that was the clue. Now you and I are finally alone, so we can begin talking."

With my situation, I had very little chance at escape. I'd need to wait this out. There was no reason not to be levelheaded despite the obvious murderer sitting in front of me. I could barely concentrate on him though. My mind was still wrapped up knowing that I'd have Angie's blood on my hands for the rest of my life.

"Where is she? Where did you put her?"

"Angela?"

"Don't be coy, you prick. Where is Angie? You can't just get rid of a body like that so easily."

"You're right. I had help."

My eyes opened more fully than they'd ever been before, and his words rang in my ears.

"Help?"

"Ah, ah, ah. Not yet. You don't get to know that yet. First, I need to tell you a story, my dear."

"Don't you dare. Don't you fucking even dare, Richard. You don't get to say my name, her name, or Bobby's. It was you who killed him. There's not a doubt in my mind now."

"Oh please, that was just the first step, Moira. Don't be such a Sherlock. For once, just listen. Bobby always told me you were great at listening. So play the silent wife and let the man talk."

"You're a—"

Before I could finish my burst of rage, a slap across my head brought back the fading haze.

"No, you listen to me, bitch. Shut up. You are going to listen, and if I need to keep hitting you senseless until you hear it, then I will do so."

I looked up at the devil who had been hiding in plain sight for most of my life, and I remained silent. Let his ego give me all the details. That might be my only way out of all this.

"Okay...I-I'm listening."

"Good."

Richard turned to move back toward Bobby's chair, the shades were closed shut. I doubted anyone had the slightest idea as to what was unfolding in my home. Richard snapped his fingers twice. Following the motions, I caught the sound of footsteps from the back of the house moving toward us. The snap must have been a signal of sorts. Richard then took his seat on a false throne and began his insidious, utterly egotistical speech.

"I made a deal, Moira. Let me tell you something first, you know, before we get into all the juicy details."

The footsteps remained on the approach.

"I've loved you since I laid eyes on you, Moira Ash. Bobby... heh. His name is feeling heavier than it ever has before. Moira, all of this could have been avoided if only you had chosen me."

He was delusional. He was really pleading to me. He killed my best friend and my husband. The selfish motherfucker.

"So after the four of us became friends and Bobby and you started seeing each other, I felt doom approaching. I needed to have you, but I could see that the hope that I so childishly held onto was a daydream that would never be fulfilled. On the day that you two were married, I sat in anguish as I was pressed further into a trap. Angela was confining, sheltered, unadventurous, an absolute bore. I needed it to go on because without her, I couldn't be close to you. As you knew a few weeks ago, Bobby and I were in a bit of a...we were drunk. Thoughts deep down surfaced, and he heard it all. Bobby was the first to hit me. You probably would have joined in if you were there. The bartender luckily broke us up before Bobby could make his final blow. Bobby was ready to kill me that night. I could see it in his eyes, Moira."

"He should have."

"I thought I told you to be quiet! Let me finish!"

As Richard went to get up and hit me again, I barely noticed that the footsteps had stopped. A tall figure clad in white gripped Richard's shoulder and, with the slightest stroke, placed him back down.

"Enough."

I looked up to the figure, and I saw him. I was not able to distinguish the type of mask he was wearing, but everything else appeared completely custom in appearance. I would know. I was a wedding dress designer. The figure then turned to me after he released his grip on Richard.

"Moira Ash, listen to this half man."

"Half-man?"

Richard then stood in anger to face the man. "What the fuck do you mean by half man?"

The figure towered over Richard, and I saw him take a step forward as Rich took one back. He was scared.

"You think to question my word choice, boy? After all that I have given you?"

"You never gave me shit! She doesn't even know why you're here. I haven't even explained that part yet!"

"Silence."

Richard lifted the gun off the table and drew it toward the man.

"I'll shoot. I don't need you after this. I just need to convince Moira."

"Shoot, boy. Do you really think that a pathetic tool will stop me?"

As I watched the two of them argue, I realized that the zip ties had disappeared. How was that possible? They were there, then they just went. *Moira, stop. Don't think about the reason. Only form a plan. Get your head straight.*

In an instant, Richard fired. I didn't know whether the shot was deliberate or...

"Ha. Ha. Ha. You stupid, stupid child."

The figure remained true. I looked at the wall directly behind him, and I saw the bullets lodged onto it. Richard either missed, or it went straight through the ghostly presence. The figure moved toward Richard, and the gun continued to fire those muffled rounds into the character. He remained on course, unwavering in his pursuit. Richard's eyes were struck with fear as each step backward was another empty shell. Finally, his back pressed against the wall. The tall man simply stood over him. Richard slid himself down the wall and cowered in fear.

"To think I made all of this happen just for this pathetic whelp." He then looked to me. "Moira, this man has forfeited our deal. You are free to walk free. Or if you so wish, you may take action against the killer of your husband and sister."

I was speechless. I knew the ties were no longer restraining my body, so I stood from the wobbly chair. I walked over to the cowering Richard, who continued to pull the trigger with only an empty clack to be heard. The primal urge inside me wanted to act out and kill the man who had destroyed my life in just a few short days, but I looked to the stranger in the room instead.

"Why?"

He looked at me.

"This half man made a deal with me. Richard's truth? He has 'loved' you since his worthless eyes were graced with your presence. He wholly believes Bobby, your husband, never deserved you. He had the impression that Bobby swept you away from him. So the night after their debacle, his shameful truth fell onto your husband's ears, and he was beaten and bloody outside of the bar, wondering what could be done. So he called upon me."

"Who are you?"

"I am called by many names, but you may call me Mr. Jacket."

"Jacket?"

"This is the name I have chosen, yes."

"Why did you offer him any deal if you knew what was going to happen? This man is a delusional and selfish murderer!"

"I suggest your tone settle in my presence, Moira. I don't take kindly to threats, as an example is present in front of you."

I looked down at the groveling Richard. He was even weeping now. I wondered if it was the guilt or the fear eating him away.

"The deal I made with this half man was a simple one. I never provided Richard the means as to which he has enacted this, well, a quite foolish plan. All I did was reveal the truth to him. He chose to accept the truth in a very perverted and warped manner."

"What truth would that be?"

"That your heart was capable of loving more than one person. It's a cradle for anyone and everything deserving of your gifts."

"So, his perversion was to rid my life of all I loved so he could have it all?"

"Yes."

I looked down at the pathetic man now pleading at Jacket's feet, but the anger was no longer bubbling at the surface. Instead, something more...*primal* was about to take control.

"Do you understand now, Moira? I know you have suffered a great deal at this man's expense. So I will offer you something in return."

I didn't even think to hesitate before the words slipped out.

"What is your offer?"

"What do you want? Right now. What is the truth that is creeping to the front of your mind? I can see it quite clearly, but I need you to admit it, Moira."

"I want to kill him. He's taken everything away from me. I have nothing left now, except a dead friend on my floor, a worthless human who has zero respect for humanity, an offer that I so clearly want to take..." I now faced Jacket. "But something deep down inside me doesn't want me to. I think that's Bobby's voice telling me not to go down that path."

Jacket approached, his hand motioning outward, and a knife of bone and silver began to mold from his hand.

"I have come to learn that the truth about this world is frightening. There is a reason I wear this mask, Moira. Behind it lies my truth. Your truth, the one you have just revealed to me, has convinced me that the truth may not always be so black and white. Your choice seemed simple, but your faith in yourself and humanity is repressing that all-too-human urge..."

I continued to watch his hand as the knife then began to transform once again. As the bone and metal bent and twisted, a rush of green and white spread into a thing across the same palm.

"To destroy. In doing this, you have reminded me that some of you are still capable of accessing something that I gave up long ago."

A white-petaled rose now lay in his palm. He moved his hand toward mine.

"W-what is this? What does all this mean? I…I…"

"Moira, you will never be burdened by this half man again. You will go to sleep and wake up anew. Your pain and regret will be gone. I cannot give you the lives of your sister and husband. I can only ease that pain. Within a petal of that rose, there is an inscription. When you're ready, read the inscription aloud. I will come."

I had so many questions, but I could not speak. I picked the rose from the stranger's hand, and I cradled it in mine. When I looked up, everyone was gone—Richard, Angie, the gun. All of it disappeared. My home, once radiant with light, was as quiet as the deepest crypt. The urge to fall asleep was setting rapidly, and I began to walk back upstairs. As I took each step toward my chambers, I scoured the surface of the rose for the inscription the man spoke of. Before the clock ticked, I must find the engraving. It was deeper than just an urge, and my body wasn't stopping.

At the top of the staircase, I was only a few feet away from my bedroom before I was put to rest. As I peeled back the last petal, I saw it, written in shining silver. I reached for the door handle and opened it. My room was the same, and my body spent no hurry moving toward my bed. Time had transitioned once again, at the whim of a petal peel, no doubt. As I read the inscription in my mind, I tried to decipher what it entailed. My body laid itself on the bed, and my eyes began to shut. As the last thought crossed through the mindscape, I started to feel at ease. The suffering appeared to be drawing its curtain. As my hand fell toward the table next to my bed, I set the flower down.

Sleep, I might finally sleep.

Fin

Chapter 8

Sack Lunch

"I'm breaking the rules by talking to you."

"What rules?"

"You know, the ones Megan made."

"Megan made rules." I was quite sure Sydney here was a *drone*. "Rules about not speaking to me?"

"Yes, Hannah. Megan's the best, so she decides. Oh, and she also said whatever your mom packed you for lunch today needed to be delivered to her, personally. She also wanted to mention the sausage and pepper sandwich she took last week was almost perfect, but make sure to tell your mom, 'No mustard this time.'"

Wow. They didn't even know. They just assumed Mom made the sandwich. She hadn't been around the last few years.

"Yeah, I'm going to have to say no to that. I'm busy. Oh, not to mention, it's my lunch."

"You can't say no to Megan."

"Says?"

"..."

"Exactly. Pull your head out of your ass, Sydney. Just because Megan's the queen bitch, or whatever the hell she calls herself, doesn't mean she tells us what to do. She just *uses* you. Think about it. You're just a messenger, one that's controllable."

She stared with a blank face. The profound message that just shattered her little monkey brain hadn't quite settled. I was quite proud of myself. It felt great to let loose on someone every so often. In all seriousness, you're probably wondering how Sydney came to the here and now. Well, let me put it to you this way: HIGH SCHOOL SUCKS.

Plain and simple. It's a bunch of growing, annoying, and oh, do I want to smother some of the teenagers. Anyways, there was Megan Bush; she was the supposed queen around these here parts, but I wouldn't place myself under her jurisdiction. I was just the punk chick who wanted to get by unnoticed and unbothered. That was not to say I didn't sneak around. Anyways, when Sydney Swain came to see me under my tree and decided to bother me by unloading this bull, I was thinking about Joy Division's second album.

Well, it certainly makes me want to murder the world.

God, she was so *stupid*, but it was not her fault. She was just innocent. I mean, her mother was a religious zealot who happened to stress control above all else. This poor girl. I most likely just destroyed her confidence, even if there wasn't much to begin with, but it was okay. She would have years to get it back.

"All right, are we done here, or are you going to just silently stare with a blank expression, Sydney?"

"..."

"You really are a sheep. When you're in fifth, say hi to Brendan for me. I'm out."

"B-b-but w-where are you—" she finally spoke.

"Out. Away. Far. From. Here."

I picked up my books alongside my backpack I had thrown off earlier when I finally tuned out the nagging girl I was leaving behind. It was all about perspective, I guess. Sydney was not the problem. In fact, she was not even a wrong person for bothering me. I was just not a *tolerable* person. My tolerance for bullshit was lower than the ninth circle of hell. Most of the time, it was just my music and me. Headphones hugged around my ears, hood pulled up, walking with no intent. The usual "leave me alone" kind of look. When the school year up and started yesterday, I wasn't too excited to entertain the thought of indoctrinating children through institutional means. So I chose to be a woman ahead of her time and get the hell away from this place. I ditched yesterday, and today's plan was the same. Dad didn't care too much. Even last year, when the truant officer brought me to his attention, he just grabbed a smoke and pulled me inside the house. No words, no hitting, not a single care in the goddamn world. I thought he'd rubbed off on me quite well.

I decided to hit the local diner for a stack of pancakes and black coffee. I was craving something sweet to get rid of all the stink just laid on me. I swear, just walking in the vicinity of that place bred stupidity. The diner was a brisk ten minutes away, and the breeze was light today. Fall hadn't really kicked in yet. The heat from the sun soaked into my clothes as the black reflected nothing back from its surface. Perfect, endless black. I quickly upped the pace when the thought of syrup seeping into pancakes and sipping on black coffee while I stuck up the place would be perfect. It was not my fault I forgot cash. Wasn't that why they put them in the drawers?

At the diner, I sat down at my usual spot at the bar. Teddy, my normal waitress, worked the next few days in a row. Teddy seemed to be the only person who understood me. She poured the coffee, grabbed me the paper, and even gave me extra syrup. She was beautiful but straightforward. We needed more people like her, but the world couldn't help but churn out more stupid children.

"The usual today, Hannah?"

"Yeah, Teddy. I'll take black coffee as well. The roast is dark today?"

"You betcha, kiddo. Say, aren't you supposed to be in school?"

"You asked that yesterday, and it's still the same answer today."

"Hannah, honey, does your pop know? You know I see him when he comes from his late shift."

Dad rarely came home anymore. He spent his nights here, talking with Teddy. Ever since Mom left, it had been mostly me living in that lonely house. Dad could barely step foot in the place without wanting to burn the place down.

"Yeah, he knows..."

There was a moment of silence, one that hurt the longer it went on.

"I'll get that order right in for you, Hannah."

"Thanks, Teddy."

I opened up the paper, and the world was up to its usual bullshit. A few deaths here, a few deaths there, politics destroying innocent constituent lives, diseases spreading from third-world countries...it wouldn't stop. This place was...it was just so broken. I thought about all the anger that built up inside, and after the years I'd been here, it hadn't fazed me in the slightest. We were broken things trying to fix a broken world. There was just no other way to look at it.

I heard the doorbell ring, waking me from my meditative state, and I turned in my seat. There he was...Officer Claremont.

"Hannah."

"Officer Claremont."

"Aren't you supposed to be in school?"

Why does everyone keep asking me the same damn question? Is there nothing else a kid can do besides go to school?

"No. I think I'm supposed to be right here."

"I'm going to need you to come with Hannah."

"What if I say no?"

"Then I'm going to have to arrest you. I know your dad wouldn't be too happy about that."

How would he know what dad cared about?

"The answer's still no, Officer Dickbag. Now leave me alone. I have a paper to read."

Teddy came out of the kitchen, holding my order in her hands. She saw Officer Claremont yet continued to bring me the order.

"Peter, how are you today?"

"Great, thanks for asking, Teddy. I'll just be taking Hannah back to school and be out of your hair quickly."

"Did she do something wrong?"

"She ditched school again."

"I don't believe that's against the law in this state, Pete. She is seventeen, almost eighteen, and I think she can make her own choices. Isn't that right, Hannah?"

Teddy knew me too well. She was practically my surrogate mother since the real one left.

"I think that's right, Teddy. Piss off, will you, Peter."

He tipped his hat and left in an unpleasant mood. He knew he came here looking for trouble. Bet he didn't think I'd give it back to him.

"Thanks again, Teddy."

"It's your life, kid. I would hate to see you get into any trouble, you know."

"Yeah...I know."

The hours flew by in the diner: I finished the paper in the first hour and slowly ate the stack of pancakes over the course. The coffee was always full. Bless Teddy. Now the sun was starting to go down on the day, as it did come the fall. I still hated it when it got dark early. It was not because I was scared of shadows; it was just the sun was the only bright thing these days. I packed up my things and left the twenty on the counter. Teddy knew to keep the change. I'd be back tomorrow anyway, no need to say goodbye. I exited the diner, and a frigid breeze blew against my face. I forgot to bring my beanie. I didn't think it would be this cold until a month from now.

Home was about a twenty-minute walk from the diner, so I picked up the pace a little. I remembered to bring a jacket, but the howling wind was messing up the music playing in my ears. I carefully selected those melodies to rid the melancholy away. Yet the music continued to fade in and out as the howling persisted. The one bit of happiness in my life was taken from me once again. Thankfully, the walk flew by, and I stepped onto the front steps. The loud creak of the wood flexing under my little weight was always the first reminder when I came home. Dad couldn't even step on it; he was also tired of repairing the damn thing too many times to step on it anymore. As I went to place my key into my front door, I noticed the door was ajar. Thoughts stabbed my brain, and my adrenaline kicked in. I was preparing for the worst. I pressed the door open and made myself known, "Whoever's in here, show yourself!"

Silence followed. I contemplated waiting in the doorway, just in case anything happened... The neighborhood hadn't been a nice one. That was pretty much all there was to this place—emptiness and crime. The neighbors could see if someone tried anything, but they would never report it. I stared down my hallway, but nothing was there. Not a bit out of place by my eye. I slowly took a step inside and quickly darted my eyes to the TV room on the right. Dad's chair was still facing the old set, and the radio was still humming; all was well in here. I moved to the kitchen, and I heard of a rummaging of things. The opposite of running stabbed my thoughts as I turned the corner. Then I saw him…Dad. He was drunk. Didn't hit the diner after his shift. Wonder why he came home?

"Dad?"

He turned toward the nagging sound, I assume, and stumbled a little. He was a tank type, but tonight, he was over his usual limit.

"H-h-hunuh, ho-oney…can y-you give me…bottle."

I turned my back on him as I looked at the counter behind me. There was a handle of whiskey sitting ready for him to pour another. Is this the night, I wonder, the night he was not going to stop? The night he was going to die from too much? I didn't know, but it felt like it.

"No, Dad. I think you should go to bed. Get some sleep, all right. This isn't going to do you any good."

"Whuh do ya m-mean? I-it's my medi-icine."

"Jesus, Dad! Get a fucking grip. She's gone. She's not coming back, okay! Stop wasting your life away. It's like you've forgotten everything! Yourself! Me! Me, dammit! I-it's like…it's like we both left that day, it seems."

In his drunken stupor, his expression turned from confused to raw emotion. I'd like to think I broke through this time. The yelling, it had a purpose. It worked for that short time, but in the morning, he was going to forget. He stumbled toward me, tears rushing down his cheeks, and reached for me. I lifted my arms up and took the hug. This was the first time we'd had a conversation since last week.

I walked him to his chair so he could fall asleep to his black-and-white Westerns, while I decided to call it a night. I headed up to my bedroom and closed my door. I saw my bed and aimed dramatically. I couldn't even bother to pull the sheet down or take off my clothes. All I wanted to do was just lie there and look at the ceiling. It was blank, much like tomorrow. There was not much to look forward to anymore. Tomorrow would be the same as today and so on—an endless cycle of new, useless time.

The sun peered through my shades and perfectly touched my eye. It was quite awful that this occurred because I looked at my clock, and it read 6:30 a.m. Yup, too early. Then I chapped my lips and noticed they were really chaffed, and now I must get out of bed and get water. This annoyed me more because I shouldn't have to wake up until "whenever I want to." But no, the sun must have entirely touched my... *Oh god...no, please no...*

"Daddy..."

I ran to him as fast as I could, and the sad thing was, I left him exactly where I left him. His hand folded across the arm of the worn leather and drooped in utter silence.

"I-I don't want to believe... He couldn't have. I hid all the..."

I halted and saw him, eyes closed, but at rest. The tears swelled, and my throat tightened. I wanted to tell him that I love him, and I wanted to hear him say "I love you too." But he was not here anymore. I hugged him, but he didn't hug back. A breath exited but made no sound. Then the sum of it hit me: I was all alone.

I lay there next to him, holding his now cold hand. My lips were still chapped. I hadn't cared to move an inch since I saw him. I didn't even think of picking up the phone. I could still smell the liquor on his breath, and the smell reminded me why I hate it so much. I always thought that was why Mom left. I always told everybody I didn't know, but hey, I lied. Nobody would understand anyway, so what was the point of trying to communicate?

At first, I thought it was something falling off a shelf upstairs, but my hearing was bad. Then the second knock came through, and that one was much closer. It was the door. Someone was knocking on the door. I juggled in my head about who it could be, but the wrong damn thought came first. She wouldn't be the one standing behind the door. I couldn't forget that Mom left us. The last splinter of hope broke again. I rose from holding my dead father's hand and went to the door. I didn't care anymore. If the end of the world lay behind the door, I couldn't care. This life could take whatever it wanted now, even me. I was tired of this pain.

I reached for the handle and felt the rush of cold shatter across my body; that was about the only feeling I had anymore. Then someone I'd never seen before who almost blended into the fresh snow from last night was standing right in front of me.

"Hello?"

"Good morning. Is your name Hannah Moore?"

His voice was sharp, but mine was became just as cold.

"Who are you?"

"You may call me Jacket, Ms. Moore. Now please, if I may request, may we take this meeting inside. I am aware of the occurrences in your house if that helps settle the request."

How could he know what happened? That was not human.

"You're quite right, Hannah."

"Did you just read my thoughts?"

"No, I simply just know what you're thinking. Now I have an offer for you that I shall only give once. Would you hear it or not?"

"What's the offer?"

"May I come inside? I need to see your father."

"I thought this was about me?"

"Oh…it is."

He approached me, and I didn't hold him back. He was not threatening. He was polite and unexplained. He was how Dad used to be. I wondered if he knew Dad. Did Dad call him before he…

"No, he couldn't have."

Then the stranger rudely interrupted my thinking.

"Would you care to hear my offer now?"

"Would I have let you in any other way?"

"Hah. You are quite the rebel, young Hannah. I'll give it to you freely then…"

He went to kneel by my dead father's side as his voice shivered down to my core, "Do you want to feel anything anymore?"

"Feel? Anything? What do you mean by that? Are you talking about making me not feel this? This damn pain that strikes me down every day I wake? This pain of waking up to my father drink himself to death, despite my doing my best to hide the liquor? Or the fact that I should've stayed up and watched him knowing I could have saved his life? He could still be here then!"

"Oh, yes. Yes, yes, yes. Now that is the *truth*, Hannah. I can take away all that and more. You'll never feel pain, fear, regret, nothing. It will be perfect, and to make it more perfect, you already know the truth about yourself. That's profound, Hannah. That's unrelentingly perfect."

What was the point of it all anyway? To experience all this before you turn into an adult. To live a life full of suffering, only for it to continue after all the cards had been dealt with. It was going to continue no matter what I chose, no matter my answer. So why would I want to keep on feeling all that again? I had the choice to do it all over.

"Okay."

Even beneath the mask he wore, I saw the slight push of it upward. He was grinning underneath, I could tell. I told the truth. What harm was there in that? I couldn't be punished for lying, right?

"Excellent. Word is the truth, and the truth is spoken. Hannah, darling, I only ask that you continue believing in the truth. For it will set you free. Now sleep."

The edges faded too quick for me too, and I was falling into emptiness.

I awoke to the cold floor, the same room. I'd like to think that it was all a dream, but my dad's still body remained in the chair. I did notice, though, that I couldn't really think what to feel right now. Was *feel* even the right word anymore? I reached up to touch my face, and there was not much. I felt a tingle, almost faint. There was contact but no touch. I walked over to my father, and I looked at him. His skin had gotten grayer. It was cold and still. But I didn't care, not anymore. Jacket gave me what I wanted—a second chance without pain.

I went back to bed but woke up shortly after. With the sun still peaked around two in the afternoon, I decided to head to the diner. Coffee sounded great, and we didn't have any here anyways. The walk was quick, and I couldn't quite comprehend how it was so fast. It was like I stepped outside my house, and voilà, I was here. That was convenient. I stepped inside the diner, but Teddy was not working today. Huh, she must have called out sick. Oh, and to my right was Officer Claremont, the silly officer who thought he could control everything. Guess what, no one was in control. It was all just chaos.

I went to my usual spot and pulled up the paper sitting on the counter in front of me. I hadn't noticed anyone working. It was just Claremont and me. I decided to spark a conversation.

"Good afternoon, Officer."

"Shit, Hannah? Aren't Saturdays the day you go out with your dad? Never seen you in here before on the weekend."

He was right. I guess I just forgot, being that Dad was dead and all. Oh, that gun looked interesting. I used to hold Dad's when he was passed out drunk. It always made me consider the weight of one's life. It was worth about an ounce of metal. Then I noticed him turning toward me, and he took a seat on the chair next to mine.

"Say…Hannah, I know we've not always had the most pleasant of exchanges…"

And there it was. What was with creepy old men thinking they could touch whatever the hell they wanted? It was time someone teaches them what it was like to feel powerless—powerless, even with the knowledge that no matter what you say, the man always wins. That gun looked even shinier now, so I decided to lure him in even closer.

"Pete, come on. You know I've always had a thing for older guys…"

As his hand began to slide up my pants, he barely noticed mine on his gun. I wondered how it was going to feel when I shoot his dick off.

Bang.

"Arghhh, Jesus, fuck! You fucking slut, I'm going to—"

Bang.

"Shut up and die."

I unloaded the rest of the clip into his corpse. With every new entry hole, a masterpiece began to come together. Each splatter of red and black, followed by the textured skin flying, was almost perfect. My own Mona Lisa.

I looked up from my work, and in the corner, I saw the man who made all this possible. He removed his mask, and for the first time, I saw his face. That familiar wink from earlier looked even more beautiful without the mask.

"Are you happy, Hannah?"

"Happy? Who said I wanted to be happy?"

Fin

Chapter 9

Best There Ever Was

They would tell you things when you were younger—things that you might not necessarily relate to or understand at that time. Things change, and they change faster than anyone of us could ever predict. Hell, look at who I am now compared to who I was ten years ago. It had been a good life, a hard but good life. After losing my son and sweetheart a few years back in a car accident, I wasn't quite sure what I'd do with the rest of my life. I knew there wasn't a point to quitting; they would have wanted me to push on. So that was what I did. I pushed on. I found another purpose in my life.

Before the war, I was a boxer. Fought in the ring fifty-two times, with almost a perfect record. My last couple of bouts weren't the best, but my mind was focused on entirely different situations than winning in the ring. Especially during that time, professional athletes or not, most of us were drafted into the war. It was the inevitability of things. We were pawns in an ideological war for domination, nothing but scrap for the elites to throw aside for the betterment of the world. In those jungles, I lost myself. I lost my sense of being. The urge to fight and kill everything in that swampy place was all I felt for a long time. I'd been fighting my entire life and hadn't taken a pit break since I came running out of my mother. Dad was a boxer too, and he started throwing punches at me when I was four. I knocked his ass out once. After he laid his hand on my mother, I decided I was fed up with his drunken bullshit. I was only thirteen when I clocked that fucker clean. He was flat on the floor for a couple hours.

Mom and I left the house that day. Soon after, I began boxing under a new coach. Billy Brand turned my life around, but that changed out there. Nothing was the same after the war. In that wasteland, I killed, shot, stabbed, burned, scalped, broke, and butchered over fifty Cong. I wasn't proud of it, but my higher-ups were. They gave me the nickname Phantom. The boys would joke around preaching I was a phantom reaping through those fields. Stupid name if you ask me. All I cared about was making it home, and if that meant killing my way through this jungle under the guise of fighting for my country, then so be it.

The war ended. We lost, and I returned home. When I came back, I brought all the violence along with me. So I directed all of it toward the guys in the ring with me. Poor bastards. Billy was becoming worried, and I was becoming everything I feared. I was turning into my father, a drunk fighter hell-bent on dishing out pain. That all changed when I met Selena. Billy and I were out one night grabbing a pizza after training, and I was beaten. I was wailing on the guys so hard that day I was pretty sure I was a bull fighting a matador; the bull was winning every time, and the matador was begging to be pulled from the field. Anyways, with my stomach growling and my hands bloodied and bandaged, we ordered our pizza, then I heard the door ring from someone coming in. I turned around, and there she was. As the French liked to call it, *un coup de feu* hit me like a gunshot, and I was struck by magical lightning—the lightning of love. All the anger that was swelling inside felt a quick jab and pushed itself back just the slightest amount. My jaw was still wide open when she spoke to me, "You going to fix up that look, big guy?"

Embarrassed, I couldn't believe this stunner was talking to me. Hell, I'd never been knocked out in the ring, but this sure as shit felt like it.

"Well?"

"My god, y-you're gorgeous."

"A compliment. Unexpected. Thank you. Are you finished ordering? My friend and I are starving, and we would like to order some pizza."

"..."

"Are you finished ordering, mister?"

I awoke from my jaw-dropped haze. "Here, here, let me get you gals your pie for you."

She didn't respond. Instead, she looked at the friend beside her. They exited the building to talk outside, and I was left quaking in my britches. The door's bell rang once again, and the two of them entered.

"Sure, but only if we can sit with you."

I swore that was the moment I knew. I had completely forgotten Billy had been with me, and he was just silently laughing inside his pulled-up jacket. I didn't think he'd ever seen me on my tiptoes like that before. Hell, I couldn't believe it myself. The butterflies in my stomach were trying to fly up and lift me to the ceiling, but I had to keep myself grounded for this lady.

"What are you laughing at, Billy?"

"Nothing, mate. Just order the pie, and let's find a table. Evening, ladies, glad for you to be joining us." Cool as a cucumber Billy was.

The voice of an angel spoke and placed her hand out to shake mine. "Pleasure." As I reached to shake her petite hand, she looked up at me and winked. She was trouble from the start, but the all-too-good kind. So we ordered the pizza and had proper introductions. Her name was Selena, and her friend was Maggie. Maggie had a thing for older guys, and Billy was feeling himself. I thought he took a few swigs from his flask on his so-called "bathroom" breaks to gain some of that courage. The funniest thing about the entire time we were there? Selena and I barely spoke a word; that was on purpose. She and I devoured most of the two pies, and we kept silently exchanging glances while the two next to us were gabbing their mouths off. We knew Maggie and Billy were going to be talking all night, so Selena and I pulled the bathroom quote. They didn't even notice us getting up from the booth. So we took that as our chance to escape and really talk. Outside the parlor, I asked where she lived, and she said she wanted to head to my place instead. I hadn't been with someone in a long time, but I didn't feel pressured to sleep with this gal. I just wanted to stare into her eyes and get lost in that ocean. She told me years later that she never felt a single worry or unnerving anxiety around me, ever. She was my perfect angel. We didn't even sleep together until three days after our meeting. The best part of those entire three days? She spent those seventy-two hours with me. We had known each other for years from the way we knew how each other moved, talked, and quirked. It was a breathtaking trip. Soon after that, I proposed, and she said yes. I was still boxing at the time, and she was fully supportive of my career. She lifted me up in every bout and was there for every round, no matter how bloody they got. I knew she was only doing it because of me, but she was a fighter as well.

Selena grew up in an identical fashion. Her father was a bastard just the same and was locked in the joint when Selena was only twelve. He crossed the line. Selena's dad had killed her mom during a fight in the kitchen. He pleaded to the judge that it was an accident, but he knew damn well which way to hit her. To have that specific a result was no coincidence. I wished my baby never had to see that, but it was okay. She told me early on about all this, and those ghosts had long since been lost to her. She was a free woman, and she lifted me higher than anyone else. She lifted me out of my own tragedies. Year after year, she jabbed and pulled those ugly pieces of hate and killing rooted deep inside me. She took that all away and helped make me the man I always wanted to be.

Ma always told me there would be three moments one would remember for the rest of their lives. I never quite understood what that meant when I was younger, but as I grew up, I gained that perspective. One of the wisest sayings my mother told me when I was heading off the war was this: "Every man has three moments in their life that they will never forget. Every mother will also have the same. Today, I'm on number 3. You're but a baby, James. You will discover the world and all it holds. Not all of it is nice, but sometimes the ugly exists for a reason. Serve your country, return home, and never forget I love you." She left me with advice that I couldn't figure out till a couple of years ago. My three days would come to be all used up since she told me that. My ma passed away when I was deployed. Her last memory of me was a perfect moment for her, and I was left suffering on the other side of the ocean, killing just to kill. The first moment was when I met Selena. The second was the day she gave birth to our son Jason, and the last was the day they were taken from me.

There was something fucked up about this world, and I'd always known it. No matter how close I was to that ultimate happiness, someone had to just go and rip it all away for no goddamn reason. Thank God for Selena. After all those years together, I knew she would have hated to see me like this. Gradually, I changed. Slowly but surely, I would honor the deaths of the people I loved by taking that killing, the rage, the anger and putting it somewhere useful.

That was why I reopened the boxing school. I opened it up in the spirit of Selena and my childhood phantoms. I created a safe space for kids to take out their rage but also learn to control it through discipline and morality. If you couldn't tell by now, I'm a boxing coach at my own gym. It used to be Billy's gym. Another friend I lost. Billy died from an alcohol overdose during one of his and Maggie's party nights. He left the gym to me in his will. Selena must've compelled him to do that. Maggie and I would see each other occasionally, but she got back to her life, and I was too focused on mine.

I helped the kids box, and the train was my salvation. It had been more than a decade since I'd been in the ring myself, but I couldn't find a reason to throw a punch anymore. I'd coached a lot of talent since I reopened this place, and every one of the kids I sent back home after their sessions left with smiles that reminded me of my lady. The neighborhood was tough, but I'd made them tougher. Nobody around here, and I mean nobody, even the pushers trying to recruit my kids, knew not to talk to them. I wouldn't even need to act or speak, because they dealt with it themselves. Controlled action—that was what I drilled into them. I couldn't be prouder, and I knew Jason and Selena would be proud of what I'd made.

I'd see them soon; I could feel it in my gut. I knew that was a morbid thing to say, but the doc didn't have great news during last week's visit. I realized I hadn't seen a doctor since I returned from the war, and I'd been feeling funny exercising with the kids as of late—tired, useless, could barely stand. So I did the thing that Selena would have nagged me about and dragged my ass to the doctor. After some tests, he broke the news to me. I have stage 4 stomach and liver cancer. He predicted I had four months to live. Treatments could be given, but it would most likely just accelerate the dying process. I knew I was on a countdown, and my priority was finding the kids another mentor. They were all I had left. It wouldn't be right if I just lay down right there and died. I could have turned back to drinking and fighting, but what good would that do?

It had been a week since my visit. I'd been pushing through the pain, just like I'd always done. The kids could sense something wrong, but I couldn't find the courage to tell them. Not yet, I kept telling myself. Sounds of bags being hit rang in my ears as I just sat in solace. I was sitting in the office at three when an old friend decided to stop by.

"You have to be shitting me! Private First McBride!"

"Hey there, Phantom," he sarcastically responded.

Charles McBride and I served together during the war, and I could count how many times he'd saved my ass—twice. Charlie didn't have much luck when he came back from the war, and I heard he got wrapped into some criminal-related trouble and was sentenced to a few in the county. I guess he just got out. I wondered why he came to see me.

"Charlie, how are you doing? It's been what?"

"It's been a little, James. I spent a few years in lockup. Did some stupid shit. Shit, our CO would have kicked us in the teeth for. The war changes you, I guess. Definitely not the right way either."

"You can say that again. I heard about from a few of the other boys about all that."

"It's behind me now, James. I'm not here looking for a handout either. I got some money stashed away that'll keep me on the road for a while. You know, to settle into a new place, start a new life, etcetera. No, I'm here to tell you something, old friend."

"What's going on, Charlie?"

He went to rest alongside my cabinet when he saw the picture of us in the jungle.

"Shit, you still have this? It's even got that same bloodstain from Johnny."

ANTHOLOGY

"Wouldn't get rid of that picture for the world, Charlie. Now what's up? What do you have to tell me?"

He was silent once again, and I could tell he didn't want to tell me.

"Charlie, come on…"

"James, I'm sorry about your lady and your boy. I heard about it in prison. Chief told me how you were at the funeral after he came to visit me in the joint. He told me you were pretty shaken up. I mean, who wouldn't be? I'm sorry for your loss, man, and the way they went… I wish I could have been there for you, brother. The guy who had been charged with the crime, he was in the cell next to mine. I didn't know his name at the time, but he was always talking about how he'd gotten away with a life sentence on a technicality. Well, I drilled that fucker's head into the wall I don't know how many times, and he still bragged about that shit. Anyways, since I've been released, I've kept my eye on the guy. I owe you for not being at the funeral, so I kept visiting the boys on the inside. I wanted to kill this bastard as soon as he got out of the jam. I had this whole elaborate plan to kidnap the guy and end his life for doing that to one of my boys. Then I realized that wasn't my call to make. The bastard who killed your wife and son has one more week, and he's out free. I thought I'd come here and let you know. It's your call to make if you want to put this turd into the ground, but it's gotta be you, James. I'll be by your side, but you have to want this."

They say people don't change, and most don't. I'd changed, and I knew why I did. This news, however, had brought something back that I thought I had gotten rid of a long time ago. That killing urge inside me, the one Selena had pacified for so long, it was creeping its way back from the grave, and it was hungry. Feral, violent, and unrelenting. Suddenly, I began thinking there were four moments in a man's life that he would never forget. That decision I was going to make, well, let's see where it would take me. It might just check the fourth box.

The bastard, *Tony Shtick*, was released as of 2:00 p.m. yesterday. Charlie and I had been tailing him for the past twenty-four hours, and the sleazy dirtbag had already gotten back to drinking. Hell, we even witnessed him break and enter one of the cars parked in the lot outside the bar and drive off half-cocked on tequila. He was a stain on this here earth, and Charlie and I were going to do something about it. One of the older boys at the gym, Terry, was running drills and exercises for the next couple of days while I was doing this. Bless that kid. This gave me the time to tail and observe the bastard. It helped us form a seal-tight plan of action. It was going to be a "maim, kidnap, torture, then kill" mission all in the span of three hours. It was the safest number we could come up to make it pleasurable and just long enough so he knew what he'd been doing wrong his entire life.

We followed him to a motel on the outskirts of the city, and it had 19/20 vacancies. That helps a good amount, especially since there was no surveillance Charlie and I could spot anywhere. We decided tonight would be the time we'd snatch him. It would give us the cover of night, and by the time we made it to the gym, we'd have plenty of time to make the runt hurt. We stayed parked across the street at the diner, just talking away about times past without forgetting why we were there. The waitress was kind and didn't mind us spending the amount of time we did in there. She was a cute little redhead, couldn't be more than eighteen. All I could think about was how old Jason would've been and how he'd probably be here now hitting on the gal. That helped all the bit more with what we were going to do. Sundown came quick, and we delightfully thanked Miranda, the waitress, and headed to the car. We would pull up alongside Tony's car and knock at his door. We would bust in, knock him out cold, then drag him into the trunk, all without forgetting to grab the motel keys and check out for the bastard. We couldn't leave any trail of us being there, so Charlie would drive his car to my gym. We would place it in the local pound the day after with Tony's body inside. I'd be dead by the time they found his worthless corpse, and that made me feel good inside.

As we pulled up next to the green Oldsmobile, Charlie parked and went back around the car to begin picking its lock without tripping the car horn. Meanwhile, I headed up toward the shit's door.

Knock. Knock.

"About fucking time... I ordered that pizza twenty minutes ago."

His muffled voice made my skin tense, and my fist closed tightly. As soon as the door opened, he would be out cold.

Click.

"You can forget the tip from me..." He saw me as he looked up from flipping his ones.

He was out before he could complete the sentence. It had been almost a decade since I had thrown a punch, and damn did it feel good. I threw his body over my shoulder and threw him into the back of the trunk. Charlie had already picked Tony's car open and moved to tape and tie up the shitstain. I was headed back into the open motel room to grab his key and check out for him. When I found the key on the counter, I turned around, and Charlie was already smoking a cigarette as cool as a cucumber. Always the smooth operator he was. I winked at him as I headed to the main office across the lot. Not a single car had driven by, and even if they did now, it wouldn't look like any out of the ordinary. I finally reached the office, and I knocked pleasantly. The host was sweet, and I told her I was the guest's homosexual partner. It would halt her from asking any questions. She handed me the bill, and I gave her whatever cash I found lying around in the scumbag's room. I told her to keep the change. She thanked me, and we were good to go. Once I was back outside, Charlie finished up his cigarette and fist-bumped me as we walk past each other all cool. The synchronous motion was something that brought me back to the days in the jungle—the days when I would ask the boys to go hunting for those Cong, and Charlie would be the only one to volunteer. I remember us sniping those fuckers from the tress. It was like one, two. Charlie shot, then I followed. We were ghosts in the trees. Look at us now, still ghosts to the city, dragging all those souls in tow behind us.

The drive back to the city was quiet as expected. The only sound was the tune of Van Morrison's "Wild Night," and I couldn't help but chuckle a little. It had been anything but a wild night. You would think that I would be worried, but this was routine. I arrived at the gym, and thirty seconds later, Charlie pulled into the lot around the back. I unlocked the front door, headed in, relocked it, then moved to the back to get the package. Hopefully, if we were lucky, he'd still be out cold. As I inserted the key into the back door and opened it up, Charlie was already waiting for me at the door. Tony was still out cold. Charlie quickly moved to the fight ring, where I followed and grabbed a chair along the way. As the three of us entered the ring, I looked at the preexisting bloodstains and imagined how perfect everything would unfold. I put down the chair and headed up to my office to grab all the tools. Charlie was already tying up our fellow to the chair as I headed to grab the equipment. When I looked out my office window, I saw it was already finished. Before I left my office and turned the light off, I saw the photo of Selena and Jason on my desk, and the resolve only got stronger. I lifted up the portrait, and I thought about what I would say if they were here right now, but they were not. I'd see them soon. I'd die knowing I did this for them.

I headed back down to the ring when Tony finally began to wake up.

"W-w-where am I?"

Charlie landed a gut punch. Tony coughed, and a little blood came along with it. Must've bitten his tongue. Idiot.

"You're in a boxing ring. Where else does it look like?"

As his little punk ass recovered, he looked up at me, and that old crooked smile I would get from torturing those Cong guys during the war showed itself once again. He didn't even need to speak. The fear wouldn't let him. He was frozen, helpless, just like my wife and son when he chose to drunk drive. Charlie wailed on him for a little, making sure he stayed conscious while I unboxed my tools. The toolbox had three simple items: a crowbar, a baseball bat, and an electric drill. I thought I'd start with the drill. As I turned the drill on and pressed the trigger, it spun so cleanly that I was mesmerized by its fluidity. Charlie then stepped away because he knew it was my turn.

I knelt down in front of the crying little prick, and I gave him the last words he'd ever hear.

"Do you remember the woman and the boy that you killed in that car accident? That was my wife and kid. You took my life away from me that night, so that's what I'm going to do over the next couple of hours. I'm going to slowly drill, beat, stab, and punch out every bit of fight and life you got in you so you can feel the pain that I've harbored for so long."

He just stared at me; he was dumbfounded. The tears rolled down his cheek, and he lowered his head. He knew he deserved this; he wasn't even putting up a fight. I was sure whatever buzz he had going was long gone, so now it was just pain. He didn't even try to say sorry because he saw my eyes. There was nothing left in them, and he knew there was no pleading with me.

I started by drilling onto both his kneecaps and the multilayers of duct tape wrapped around his raisin-like head, barely letting out a sound. He passed out for a quick second, but then I woke him up with a few chemicals to spark his brain up. He wouldn't go out that easy. Charlie then grabbed the bat and smashed it over the guy's hands and arms. Splinters of bone and muscles were starting to rise to the surface. His tears had stopped coming, and I was sure drops of blood were going to follow shortly. We were careful to start from the outside then move in so we wouldn't risk killing him too soon. After Charlie finished by breaking both of the guy's arms, I grabbed the crowbar. I let him settle for just a second; I wanted him to see the crowbar enter into his stomach. As his head twitched upward, I dropped the crowbar and instead formed a fist. This would make it all feel better. His head now rose, and the first thing he saw was that hook that I threw my dad when he hit my mother a lifetime ago. I forgot to hold back, and I knock him clean out. Before I noticed that he was out cold, the second punch was already being thrown, but Charlie caught it. For the first time since we left the diner, he spoke, but it was not his voice.

"Bravo, James. Bravo!"

I quickly withdrew my arm from Charlie's grip and took a step back.

"Charlie, are you all right?"

"Charlie McBride, Vietnam veteran, criminal, now deceased. No, I don't believe you're even speaking to a Charlie."

"W-who are you? What have you done w-with Charlie?"

"James, please settle. I'm not here to hurt you. I'm only here to help."

He began to step toward me, and his chillingly sharp voice stabbed me.

"You said deceased. D-did Charlie die?"

"Yes, in prison."

"T-then how did... No! Why did you visit me?"

"Let it come back to you, James. Here, let me help."

He stepped forth, and I couldn't step back. He placed his hands on my head, and I remembered what happened a couple of days ago. He showed me what really happened. The voice was the same as it was now, but I wanted it to be Charlie. My mind wanted it to be him.

"You're dying, James, and I came to you in your hour of need. I appear to many, and your dying brain made it more comfortable for you by making me Charlie."

If it had been this man the entire time, then why was he helping me with murder?

"I-if you're really not Charlie, then who are you?"

"You may call me Jacket."

His words stabbed with each spoken note. Who was this guy?

"As I said before, James, I came to you in an hour of need, and I presented you with what you've been seeking for most of your life. A way out of the violence. A way to change who you were. But that's not the truth about you, is it, James? No. No, you're a killer, a damn good one at that. And your morality? Now that's something to be proud of! That's why I've helped you so much tonight, James. Notice who's done the heavy lifting? You and I both know you're dying, and if you tried this yourself, you would probably be dead already. In frank honesty, you told me that day, after I gave you all the information about Tony here, that the last thing you wanted to do before you died was make the, ahem, *fucker* who killed your wife and boy get what he deserved for his actions. If that's not justice, then I don't know what is!"

He was right. I could feel the sudden shortness of breath becoming quicker. It was getting harder to breathe, and Jacket was confirming that this would, in fact, be my last act.

"I have never lied to you, James. I have only revealed the truth and have helped you fulfill your last truthful wish."

Then I thought about Selena. I thought about those short flashes of happiness that we had and could have had. Now I had a choice to make. Do I follow the calling deeply rooted in my blood, or do I defy and honor my wife and all she helped me to become?

"I die tonight. That was the contract."

"Yes."

I turned to look at the man who was still a stranger to me. And I knew I couldn't choose, not really. I knew I'd see my baby and my little boy again. There was no stopping what I was, what I'd always been. *I'm sorry, Selena. I'm sorry that I can't help myself. You're not here, but I'll be with you soon. You and Jason. Then we will be together again.*

"Stranger?"

"James."

"Make sure none of the kids see this. Please, one last promise, one last matter to attend. Don't let the kids see this…what I really am."

"Certainly."

I reentered the ring, and Tony was beginning to wake up from the knockout. His eyes were glazed, and I knew he wasn't aware of what was going on. There had been too much pain over the years, so I was going to end this while I still could, my way. I let Tony know that it was going to be me, and I'd make it quick.

"This is a mercy, kid."

He nodded, and his head drooped. I grabbed his head in my hands. I made it quick, and with the flick of my wrists, I dropped his head from my hands. I felt a breath escape my lungs, and I knew I didn't have long. I stumbled onto one knee, and I looked at the stranger. He had returned to his original form, and I see him now. A tall man in white with a mask that would haunt me after I was gone. My vision was collapsing inward, and I knew it was coming. I rested in the ring, and I closed my eyes. I saw flashes of the good times in my life, and I held onto those.

I heard her voice calling as I finally lay to rest.

Fin

Chapter 10

The Man with *the Ivory Mask*

They kept me in here, locked away from the rest of the world. They said it was for my physical well-being and the safety of others. That was what the docs continued to tell me, but I thought it was a load of bullshit. I didn't do anything wrong to be kept in here. All I did was end the life of a murderous rapist.

I stopped keeping track of days well into a year of my imprisonment. Then again, I'd been imprisoned for most of my life at this point. They kept me outside the city in this "rehabilitation" center or, as I liked to call it, the center for psychotic residents. The local police were terrified that I'd run through the streets again like some madwoman, but I'd changed. It was only the one time you see. I had been forced to birth a monstrosity after I was raped and vandalized, in every form of the word.

From what I remember, I was eighteen when he took me. He was a foul-smelling beast, sweaty and covered in sores. Every time I resisted him, he would beat me till near unconscious, then he would have his "fun." I remember lying there, watching helplessly, as he kept forcing himself inside me. Blood, urine, and who knows what else were always coming out of me. I didn't even realize I was pregnant till the bump showed up. The bastard...I never even got his name, and good riddance for that. What I did remember, though, was the day I escaped from his enthralls.

I awoke to the sound of another victim, bound and gagged in the corner. He must have brought her there when I was sleeping. I remember noticing the terrifying expression permanently fixed to her face as she looked at me. She was younger than I was, even more scared and already broken… It was then I decided I wouldn't take this anymore. No matter the beating, no matter the drugs, no matter what I carried inside me, I would stop this monster from ever touching another woman ever again.

The bastard never kept a clock in the room, but I got used to telling the time based on the low level of sunlight peering in through the grate, slowly peeling off the wall from the weeds grappling onto it. All these months locked away from the world, and I had grown to observe the little things. Isolation…it's oddly funny when I think about it now. I wouldn't be who I am today without him and my time imprisoned. One thing was for sure: I'd never regret gutting him that day.

As the lost girl wept her tears away with her hands bound in rope, I crawled my way over to her. I was kept on a leash wrapped around my neck. The chaffing and scarring from my time had become invisible by this point, so the only pain I could feel was from the beating he gave me nightly. I was used to the pain there as well; I doubt I was even able to feel anymore, after all the pain I endured. I arrived at the helpless girl tied up in the corner, and I held my hands over her mouth. My throat was so swollen from the dehydration that I couldn't speak to her, so I had to find another way to communicate. I noticed the chalk on the ground, but there was barely an inch of the damn stick left. I remembered counting the days with it when I first got here, but that activity faded early on. I released my hand from the girl's mouth and flashed all the smile I could. I nodded and felt the clumpy bit of blood flow from my cracked lips. I tried to get the message across that everything was going to be all right, but I didn't think she understood. I noticed her eyes were drooped, and the black bags under them were quite noticeable. I looked down and saw her arms were poked and prodded from needle usage. He must've pulled her off the street when she was passed out from being high.

I doubt she could understand what I was trying to do, but it was no matter. That day would be my escape, and nothing was going to stop me from getting this girl and me out of there. I crawled once again to grab the chalk, and I began writing on the wall with what little there was left. With each precious inch, I wrote a simple message: "I. You. Free. Kill the man." The chalk then ran out, and I turned my head to the girl. I nodded once again, and she stared back. I hoped she understood this time, but I couldn't tell if she was still high or comprehending.

I then looked outside through the little grate protruding with the slightest bit of sunlight. I figured it was mid to late afternoon judging by the way the light entered. I knew he would be coming any minute to perform his usual rounds. Then again, I remembered thinking about how I could comprehend the way this beast thought. I just had to hope. Hope was the only thing I could anticipate at that point.

The plan had been forming in my head for quite some time. I had been able to bend and break off a piece of the metal bed frame I was forced to rest on during my captivity. Ornamented with cold grate mesh and steel piping holding each corner, I used the parts torn off and fashioned them into a weapon of sorts. I made a perfectly sharpened knife, about four inches long. I could even hide it in my palm. All I had to do then was wait for him to get close so I could stab the motherfucker till he dropped. I returned to my bed frame and kept an eye out for the entrance above. I didn't remember how much time passed, but I remember hearing the whistling as he opened the door to the basement. His smell immediately swept into the room, and I remember gagging from the stench. As he walked down the steps and made contact with me, I stared at him with a blank expression. I knew I couldn't show him any weakness; he particularly loved it when I screamed. I kept that thought in my head, knowing what I was about to do. He skipped over the new girl and headed directly toward me. As his greasy hands rubbed against my cracked skin, I remember whispering in his ear the final words, "I'm going to kill your child…"

Time turned slow, and I remember stabbing the fat bastard repeatedly through the neck. Spurts of blood splashed on my face, and I didn't care. I was covered in his fluids by the time my frenzy had stopped. His head had barely managed to remain attached as it slumped onto the ground. Blood continued to spill, and I noticed the last breath escaping his worthless body. I knew to kill him was the only way to escape, and I was happy with my work. I remember forcing myself out of bed, and I rolled his body over to grab the set of keys in his pocket. I released myself from my chains and then fumbled over the bound girl. I used the bloody shiv I had to begin cutting the girl loose. As the ropes were loosened and she could move, she lashed out at me.

Drained from the attack, I couldn't defend myself properly. The drug-crazed woman, still with duct tape covering her mouth, looked down at me as she kept hitting me repeatedly. It got a little hazy from there. Flash of red and black continued when I remember getting the upper hand. With all the strength I had left, I pushed the woman off, forcing her back into the corner. In a struggle to speak to calm her down, she then leaped once again at me. I felt my head slam against the concrete floor when I blacked out.

There was not much I remember after that. I woke up here when I found out all that had unfolded between then and now. The doctor had informed me that I had decided to go on a killing frenzy as soon as I escaped the basement I had been held captive in for so long. The druggie that had attacked me? She was found dead along with a man in his basement. Both had died from repeated stabbings to the carotid artery. The news shocked me when I really awoke from the nightmare. Apparently, after I escaped to the world outside, a neighbor had noticed my beaten body covered in blood wandering the random street. The neighbor had run out of their house to aid me. Still in a frenzied state, according to the police reports, I used the shiv once again to murder the woman who was simply trying to help me. I didn't understand. I couldn't understand. Between the blackout and my first time walking into the halls of this institution, I couldn't remember a single event. Sure, there were vague flashes of lashing out, but that was all. Between the initial arrest near the scene of the crime, the jail time, the court hearings, and my eventual sentencing, nothing rang even the slightest piece of memory.

Surprisingly, I had been placed here on a plea for insanity. The case formed against me had elected me responsible for the death of three individuals. Despite the investigation of the man who had imprisoned and raped me for God knows how long, the killing was ruled as murder rather than self-defense. The doctor and nurses who treated me with God knows what told me the stories. Some wouldn't talk; others would. And I slowly began piecing the missing blanks in my head. A week into my incarceration at the institute, Dr. Gorman explained to me that I had suffered a severe brain injury during my time imprisoned. His prediction concluded that the trauma inflicted had activated some primal human urges inside me. Thus, all the pain and suffering I had experienced would turn into an unconscious frenzy. During one of my first meetings with my doctor, I had experienced one of these frenzies, but I had zero recollection of such events. I couldn't comprehend why I would attack someone who was just trying to help me. After lashing out at my doctors, the orderlies restrained me into a straitjacket and placed me in solitary. Once again, I was alone with no one but myself and tall tales of my psychotic break.

It had been months since I'd been placed in solitary. The drugs the orderlies and nurses had me on were supposed to put me at ease, but my mind never ceased to stop. They said I was already crazy, but I couldn't help but think that the medication and solace were the ones doing the driving. Dr. Gorman had continued using the same medications, but nothing was happening. I still felt like me. I just wanted to live free of captivity. I…I didn't want to harm anybody…

The door to my cell opened, and my normal orderly, Mr. Simon, came to wrestle me up. He told me I had my weekly meeting with Dr. Gorman. I remained silent. Every time I talked, I would just get a sharp nudge into my backside, telling me to behave. Goes to show you how men with control never want to wrestle it loose. Maybe a woman's life is meaningless to these beasts called men. He escorted me down the numerous chalk hallways, and we arrived at the doc's office. He unshackled my leg bindings and pushed me in the door. I tripped and fell, and a single emotion failed to show on Mr. Simon's face.

"The doctor will be in shortly," he said.

He proceeded to then slam the door, leaving me in the only room I ever got to see sunlight. A knock followed a few minutes after Mr. Simon closed the door when I noticed the creaky white thing open. I failed to recognize the orderly walking in. H-he was wearing a mask of sorts...

"Good afternoon, Ms. Quietly. I am Dr. Jacket. I will be handling your case from here on out."

His voice creaked with cruelty. I flinched at the sheer coldness of his breath. I didn't believe it. I didn't want to believe this man was here. How could they possibly set me up with an even more uncaring doctor?

"I...I thought my doctor was Gorman?"

"It was, but Dr. Gorman has been determined to be inadequate for your case."

My case... He had to have read it; he'd be an impostor if he hadn't.

"Would you mind refreshing me on the conditions of my case?"

"Absolutely." He then proceeded to take a seat at the sole desk in the room.

No words formed as he sat and stared at me from opposing sides. I was waiting for the response, but I was caught in the gaze of his mask. It was...detailed, ornamented, precise. I-I'd never seen anything quite like it. It almost reminded me of it... Huh, I couldn't quite place my thumb on what it reminded me of. The silence continued as he finally moved to open my case file. I caught flashes of the crime scene images, and I didn't feel any recourse of emotion. Maybe there was something wrong with me.

"As I was saying, Ms. Quietly, I have determined that Dr. Gorman was inadequate for your case. I believe I have found the solution to your most interesting problem."

"W-what do you mean?"

"Putting it plainly, there's nothing wrong with you."

"I…I don't understand… Why am I here then? Why have I been charged with all these crimes? Why have I been labeled as a danger to society if I haven't committed such atrocities?"

"Please control yourself, Ms. Quietly. I know this may come as a shock, but I've determined that your actions were nothing but normal human responses. There were no malicious backings supporting what you did. In my opinion, you're as regular as the rest of us. Now I would like to ask you a few questions before I divulge any further information. Do you mind if I ask you these questions?"

I…I didn't know what to say. This…this whole time I thought I… No. I'm innocent. He's right. I shouldn't be here. This could be my only chance to escape. Just follow along. Answer the questions, Dawn, and maybe I can get out of this.

"N-no, I don't mind."

"Excellent. Now please tell me, if you can, the circumstances in which you chose to abort your child?"

The question hit me like a train wreck. I…I had… I looked down and realized I no longer bore a belly the size of a pregnant mother. It was like…it just disappeared. Why? Why was this coming up now? How could I not remember…killing an innocent…

"I-I'm sorry, Dr. Jacket, but…I don't remember."

"Of course, you do. There's no need to lie to me, Ms. Quietly. May I call you, Dawn?"

"Y-yes."

"Dawn, in my files, I have the exact time and date you decided to abort the child you carried. It happened right here in this facility last night. At 12:08 a.m., you used a confiscated coat hanger from the laundry's coat closet and mutilated the child inside of you. Security cameras flagged the action, and your orderlies removed you from your room at 12:20 a.m. from excess blood loss."

"N-no, that's not possible. I… How? How could I have done it?"

"Before we get to that, I want to ask you about the man whom you claimed imprisoned you and impregnated you with his child. Do you remember his name, Dawn?"

He jumped to the next question, but my head was still rattling from the first one. I didn't know what was happening to me. I...I just didn't remember...

"I never asked..."

"He never mentioned it to you? You were there for quite some time."

"You don't believe me. You won't believe me."

"My dear, I believe you. In fact, I took your case because I think we need more people like you."

His words splintered across my body. H-he believed me?

"Y-you believe me? I...I thought I was just going crazy... No one's believed me this en-entire time."

"Dawn, I'm a simple man. I believe people should know the truth about themselves and all of this. Those who lie deserve all the wrong in the world. Trust me when I say this. Now after asking you a few of these questions, I can conclude this is just a case of forgotten identity. There's nothing wrong with you, Dawn. In fact, I have the ability to clear you from all your charges and release you on good behavior. For all this to happen, though, you'll need to hear the truth, the whole of it."

Freedom. He just offered me my freedom from this place. This could be my second chance, the one I so rightfully deserved after all this... *Wait. It can't be this simple. Every man that's ever given me anything always requests something in exchange.*

"Why are you helping me?"

"I already told you, Dawn. The world needs more people like you."

"And what do you mean by that?"

"It's simple, actually. You rid the world of bad people who do terrible things. What makes you special, though, is that you've never lied for performing those actions. You've never convinced yourself that killing is wrong because it isn't. Let me ask you this. Do you remember the young woman who was imprisoned in that basement with you?"

He was right; I'd never lied. This entire time, people had been telling me I lied about this entire series of events. The judges, the police, my lawyer, all begged me to give it up. All tried to have me admit that I was the reason this world was so fucked up.

"Yes, I remember her."

"Did you know she was an accomplice to your imprisonment?"

"What?"

"Yes, Dawn. She attacked you not out of fear but out of anger. You killed her boyfriend, you see. The sick little addict and liar were working with your captor to help scoop up girls like you across town. She aided and embedded this man with three other cases, all involving girls like you. Girls were found raped, beaten, and buried in the backyard simply because he enjoyed it. Do you want to know why she helped him? When a girl wants dope, she's going to find it any way she can, even if that means helping out a sociopathic rapist."

"No…I…I thought I was helping her."

"You live in a corrupt and imbalanced world, my dear. You've been imprisoned, raped, beaten, defiled, and drugged for most of your adult life all because the world sought to throw a good person, like you, under the rug for simply existing. Terrifying, if you ask me. That's why I'm here. I'm here to help you see that the lies being forced down your throat no longer hold any bearing. After our little meeting here today, you will be free to roam and correct the world in any way you see fit. That is my gift to you, Dawn."

He was telling me all I wanted to hear, but I didn't see the point. He hadn't answered any of my questions.

"I want to hear it. I want the truth."

"Ah, now you're beginning to understand. Good. May I?"

He moved his hand toward his face. I believed he was asking me if he may remove his…well, his mask.

"Y-you want to remove your mask? What does that have to do with hearing the truth?"

"Hearing and seeing are two very different actions, Dawn. In my experience, showing the truth holds more ground than simply listening to it. All I ask is that you look deep and you don't stop looking until you've seen it all."

My curiosity placed itself above my cautiousness. I nodded, and he understood he may remove his mask. As he proceeded, I quickly looked at the sun glaring at us through the windows, and the warm feeling reminded us that there was still a world out there—a world I might have the chance to rejoin. I looked back at Dr. Jacket when I saw it. I saw a swarm of stars in an endless abyss as I was pulled deeper into his gaze. Oceans of infinite black washed the edges away as I was transported into the unknown. In the black nothingness, I looked around, and I saw stars shimmering and dazzling with light. I caught glimpses of my life flashing across the endless streams scattered before me as the pieces began fitting themselves together.

I pulled myself away as I had finally seen it all.

"They lied…about everything. They set me up. The man who raped and imprisoned me? He was the mayor's son. The mayor's family gave birth to a sociopathic rapist, and they covered it up when the police had discovered what they found at his house. They made it look like I was the one who captured the woman, like I was the one who raped and held them in captivity. All that evidence that clearly nailed him? Erased, burned, and destroyed. The reason why it worked? They used my traumatic head injury as the weapon so that no one would believe me. Ha. Who would believe the crazy woman? They destroyed my life, and for what? To protect a guilty, worthless human pile of garbage?"

"*They* tend to do that, especially when a case like yours hits. No one ever wants to help a woman at her weakest. They simply use her as a scapegoat. So now that you know the truth, what will you do?"

I paused to think. An itch scratched the back of my head, as I felt a thought creeping its way to the foreground. I knew what it was, but could I possibly do that?

"I'm going to kill them…all of them."

"Good girl. Please come here so I may release you from your bindings. You serve a new purpose in this life, Dawn Quietly. Now go forth into the world, reveal the truth, and let none of it go unseen."

As I shuffled my way to the man freeing me from my shackles, I stared one last time into the starry black eyes that freed me. He bowed his head and blessed me with a kiss as gentle as my mother's.

"Close your eyes, Dawn. You will awaken outside, where you will finally be emancipated from the lies."

I closed my eyes, and a rush of cold wind rushed past. I felt the sun peering down on my body as I opened my eyes. I was standing on the street. I looked back, and there it was, the prison that held me for so long. That was behind me now. Today I start anew, and I could finally go after the bastards who lied to destroy my life.

I walked down the bike lane of the two-lane highway with purpose, something that I'd been searching for my entire life. The walk to the city was a far one, but that gave me plenty of time to think about my newfound purpose, to contemplate the ways I was going to punish those who destroyed the lives of women like me. Did they really think they could keep that covered up for so long and not expect me to come after them?

I hope they beg when they see me.

Fin

Chapter 11

Blue Suite

It all started in *1326*.
    I was a simple farmer living under the duke's influence. I was a nobody in a domain meant for nobodies. I had no family, no progeny. It was just my farm and me, if you could call it even that. My role in life? Raising livestock.

One day, the duke was unhappy with my livestock output. So he decided to take a trip from his towering stone palace to come and see my little field. Once he arrived, he entered my lonely household to have a discussion. At the table from which I dined, he drilled my head down into the countertop and demanded more livestock. Of course, livestock didn't grow from trees, and it took time for sheep, cow, pig, and ass to grow. Nothing was immediate. To the duke, all he cared about was immediacy. So as he pushed my head farther and farther into the wobbling table, I submitted to his force. For what else was there for me to do besides obey?

Then events turned *interesting*. You see, people look at death, and most were frightened by it. That day, I had this crawling intuition down my spine that I would be welcomed with open arms into death. After releasing my head from the table, his troops entered my household and broke down the door. Oh well, I would never return here after this day. They wrestled with grabbing me from the table, and I did not put any struggle when they bagged my head. They dragged me through my barren field down to the river with nothing to cover my skin. Not only did they take my life, but they took my dignity as well.

My life was worth nothing, and I was welcoming expiration. *There must be something better than this,* I thought to myself. Life was better than the dirt and shit I had been thrown into. As I heard the muffled water rushing beneath me, I felt the duke's troops put weight and tied my legs together. They wanted to drown me just for the hell of it. The last words I heard before they tossed me in were these: "You will forever be nothing. You are worthless. Now enter into the sea where filth like you belong."

The crime I was being charged with? there was none. It was his will, so be it punishment come forth. That was all I was to this duke, property on his land. So I felt the soldiers press against my back, and I jumped into the rushing water. I was a lamb that jumped freely into sacrifice. What else was I useful for besides pedaling more death into the air?

As the water breached my lungs and the air escaped through tiny drowning bubbles, I embraced the pain. It was then that I died. I felt my heart slowed to a halt, my vision blurred and blotted, the sound became inaudible, shit poured from my behind, and the last light escaped my eyes. Little to my knowledge, I would be brought to a place more beautiful than any I could have ever imagined.

I woke up. There was no water. There were no chains or bindings. No noises or sounds of rushing water. Only blue and black. Blue light illuminated an all-black box. A singular door was positioned at the end of the room, and it was slightly ajar. I was sat down on a chair made of silver. Placed in front of me was a golden table. One glass, empty, set on it. In the desolate place, I felt nothing. Was I supposed to? It wouldn't matter shortly.

The door slowly began opening, and a towering figured awaited on the other side. He was drenched in white. A mask of ivory covered his face, and a cane of old oak, with a silver helm, lay between his immense figure. He spoke, and time and space halted at his will.

"Welcome, Darwyn."

"I think I'm lost. I'm not sure how I got here."

"No, you're not lost. I brought you here."

"You did?"

"Yes. Darwyn, I have a proposition that I would like to ask of you."

"Forgive me, but I don't know who you are, and as I said before, I don't know how I got here. Do please forgive me of my hesitation in answering or asking your inquisitions."

"Ah, I see. You haven't quite realized where you are. Well, let me assure you, Darwyn. You are neither dead nor alive. You are…in between. You are now an eidolon."

"An eidolon?"

"Darwyn, what is the last memory you have?"

I looked at the man questioning me, and I tried to remember what I last experienced. I couldn't seem to recall anything.

"I…I don't know."

"There's your answer, Darwyn. You are a phantom, a being with an identity, but no purpose, no substance. You will forever be this way until you listen to my proposition."

"Your proposition?"

"Simple."

As the tall man moved from the doorway to join me at the golden table, the blue light illuminating the room began to glow brighter with each closing step. He finally pulled up a chair and took a seat across from me.

"I will silence the questions in your mind while I tell you about myself."

He placed his cane against his chair, and the silver helm placed at the top reminded me of a pendant I'd seen long ago.

"I'm old, Darwyn. I have walked for a very long time. I have observed and acted where need be, but no one commands me. I am my own master, my own will. Like you, I am neither dead nor alive. I exist even when nothing exists around me. You'll learn once this conversation ends what all this means. That's the point of this entire thing—the meaning. My past should not concern you, for you have no place in it. Darwyn, tell me, what do you consider to be the truth? The truth about this existence and all that lies in it?"

As he waited patiently for my response, I was enamored by his mask—the soulless yet beautifully crafted ivory that decorated his expression. I wondered what lay beneath. Did he hide a disfigurement?

"No."

"I-I'm sorry… Did you just say no?"

"Your thoughts are loud, my dear boy. I can hear everything you're thinking."

"So you are answering the question I posed in my head?"

"Yes, would you like to see what's underneath?"

A moment's hesitation passed, but I felt compelled.

"Underneath the mask?"

"Certainly."

I nodded, and he began to remove the ivory. As his hands moved up from his side, he gently removed the mask while turned away. I waited patiently. Anxiety did not flood in. Instead, intrigue flowed through me more so. As he turned back around, I saw many a scar across the lower portion of his expression, and as I looked up, I saw…

"W-what is that?"

"Darwyn, that is the truth."

"I-i-it can't be."

"It is wholly."

"But why?"

"I never thought to ask, but maybe you will."

"I will?"

"Darwyn, I have brought you here because my journey has finally reached its end. The journey is one solely for the lone walker, one divided by the simple propositions of what is the truth behind everything. For there is no lie that will escape you. You will be a purchaser to the truth and nothing but. You will walk, and you will hunt not because you want to but because you're compelled to. Your desire will grow and grow. The truth will seek you out, but you will need to find it yourself as well. This is a gift, not a curse. I promise you that you will see more than you could possibly imagine. The life you lived already? Forget it. This is who you are now. There is no return from this, only succession. So I ask you this. Will you accept the mantle I present to you?"

"I don't even know what you are. What mantle is that you speak of?"

"All you need to understand is this: you were nothing. Everyone is nothing. All that matters, no matter the conditions, is the truth. Who you are, what you've done, what they have done to you, what will be done to you, none of that matters. This gift I'm offering you will give you answers to the questions that have riddled existence since its wretched beginning. You will be the purveyor to the truth. You will see and see further than anyone could ever dream. This mantle will need a title, and you will also bear its name. Darwyn will no longer exist, only the name you choose for yourself will matter now. Do you accept all of this and the many answers you will receive in time?"

"You have given me no answers. I demand them before I accept—"

"Boy! You do not have the right to demand of me. Have you not been listening? I am offering you the chance to become something that is wholly unique without a burden."

"If it's without burden, then why do you give it to me now?"

"I am old. I have waited a long time for an individual like yourself. My time is not mine to determine, as yours will be. There must always be a successor. That is the only answer I can grant you."

"If you can only answer in riddles and enigmas, then let me ask this. What makes me so special? I was a nobody. You even said so."

"What's more becoming? To be nothing or to become something from nothing? This is what I offer."

I knew he could read every thought that would run through my head, but it didn't matter anymore. I felt convinced, oddly. I wanted this. He was right. I couldn't go back to where I was. I was drowned after all. There was only one question that remained.

"Is revenge entailed in the occupation?"

He moved his hand to the top of his cane, and he pressed a button on the other side. As I heard a latch loosen, he moved his hand to pull on the top of the pendant, revealing a tiny scrolled parchment. He began to unravel it upon the table and pressed it toward me.

"Immortality, vengeance, truth—they are all the same. Sign below, and all will be revealed."

As I looked down on this tiny piece of parchment presented before me, I felt compelled to sign. All I needed was a tool.

"This should be adequate."

He clicked the latch one last time, and a sharp-tipped object appeared. He moved the cane toward me and told me to place my thumb along the tip. I pricked myself, and my blood did not look my own anymore.

"I-it's black."

"You no longer need living flesh."

"Will I be able to die?"

"In time, but I would not label it death. As I said, succession. Now with your hand bloodied and the parchment waiting, will you take this gift I offer?"

As the bleeding black fluid dripped from my thumb onto the rest of my hand, a sigil began to form, and I wanted to press the fluid into the parchment.

"I do."

I signed in bloody black ink.

The beginning is always the most expositional of any story, except for one such as this. The story previously stated was one from the life that I no longer had any connection to. Once I signed, I became free. It was harder to recall with the passing years, but one note was this: I will never forget my first time waking. It was *1326*.

I awoke immersed in water, and I swam upward to the surface. Guided by the light gleaming from the sun, I burst through the ceiling of water and found myself exactly where I was once murdered. I was unaware of the time past, but I would soon discover such musings.

Fin

Afterword

The Oddly True Story

I started *Anthology* while I was on a train up to Santa Barbara. I was visiting my brother for the weekend at his college apartment. We were going to catch up and do brotherly things, but that was not the moral of this story, folks. Let's backtrack a little. So there I was waiting for my train to arrive, and I saw this man dressed in an all-white suit. I'm talking *cocaine white*. This guy was wearing a fedora, bow tie, vest, button-down, cuff links, jacket, and pants perfectly put together with matching white leather shoes. Probably alligator or something absurd. It was spectacular in a fashion sense, and this struck an idea. Anyways, the first thought that ran through my head was this, *Holy shit! This guy could be terrifying, but he's too good-looking.*

What came of this seemingly random thought? *The idea for Mr. Jacket.* Simple, enigmatic, mysterious, and for any situational context, confusing as all hell. It was the outfit that began the story, then I created the endings and the characters for each story. The most important part of this blossoming idea was this: I wanted to create a character in an anthology-style universe—a universe of my own making, with seemingly infinite applications. I wanted this terrifying character to be there and sometimes not even there, but still there to scare the shit out of you and reveal the darker tendencies and truths I had seen in myself and humanity. Besides introspection, humanity is the scariest thing on this planet, and there had been evils recorded throughout the ages that were goddamn scary. So when I was creating these stories, researching some disturbing historical moments, and exploring the darker side of the human psyche, I began creating *Anthology*.

God, there were some scenes that I'd reread, and I'd question my sanity in some of those terrifying applications I remember during the mapping stages of this book. I wanted some of the situations to not shy away from the no-go zones, those terrifying tendencies that should never be exploited. I'm talking about the talk I had with my mother when I tried sharing my ideas. I think this was the turning point when I knew this could be an amazing horror anthology. And there we were at family dinner. I grabbed my mother's attention and quickly spoke, knowing my sister would soon jut in. I divulged what I had been recently working on.

"Would you like to hear about one of the horror stories I'm writing?"

There was an obvious and becomingly annoyed expression growing before she spoke, "Sure."

"Excellent. So it's about this mother and her son—" I was stopped midsentence.

"Stop!"

"What?"

Her voice became deeper. You know, "the mothering voice."

"If it has anything to do with hurting children, mothers, husbands, wives, or anything really with death, then I don't want to hear it."

"So no horror in general?"

She took a sip of her wine. "Yes."

"All right!"

Little did she know, I wrote some terrifying stories about all those things.

Sorry, Mom.

About the Author

Robert Deshaies II is a student, writer, poet, and lover of all literature. He collects comic books, graphic novels, and many poetry books. He has an obsession with early twentieth-century writers who have thus influenced his life to pursue the written works presented before you. Damn, Fitzgerald and Hemingway. He is a bookie, a lover of superheroes, the entire comic median. (Batman especially. Why? He's awesome.) Robert is also an avid coffee drinker; some say in excess amounts. He is currently developing upcoming projects focusing on screenplays, a *continuous* collection of short stories, a series of graphic novels, and of course, more poetry to sate his hopeless romantic soul.

CPSIA information can be obtained
at www.ICGtesting.com
Printed in the USA
FSHW011904241120
76243FS

9 781646 547418